The Carer

By Nigel J Williams

I would like to point out that this book is purely fictional and does not represent my personal view, or portray the professionalism and kindness shown by carers who look after our elderly, our infirm and at times sadly our dying, and who spend their lives simply caring for others.

All characters and events in this publication are purely fictitious, and any resemblance to real persons either alive or dead is purely coincidental.

1. Rebecca

Aunt Mae's Funeral – 28 March 2015 – Canford Cemetery, Bristol.

"Ashes to ashes, dust to dust, we commit this body to the grave."

The Very Reverend Arthur Brennan's hands trembled as the biting wind turned the water to ice at the bottom of the muddy pit and a first dusting of snow settled on the wicker casket. Sobbing laments echoed within the stark confines of the walled graveyard, as Aunt Mae's spirit departed this world for the next.

On one side of the grave stood Rebecca Thorneycroft – Aunt Mae's former carer –all alone, her face emotionless, her phoney sobbing largely being ignored by the grieving family standing opposite. Whispered comments behind gloved hands offer nothing but scornful glances as she stared deep into the open grave.

Despite their searing hatred, Rebecca stood resolute and unwavering in her resolve drawing on an inner resilience, trying to ignore the loathing coupled with the freezing wind blowing across the graveyard. Her jet-black hair was cut in a stylish bob then – shorter on one side, liquid and flowing on the other. Her lips were cherry red and pouty. Rebecca was beautiful. And she knew it.

Go to hell! She thought as she blew into her woollen mitts and looked across at the range of snow-speckled umbrellas and the drawn white handkerchiefs as their rhythmic wailing was lost and scattered to the icy wind.

None of you mean a thing to me. Who am I? I'm just the carer. She was an old bitch anyway and you all hated her, so stop play acting. Besides I'm much better at it than you. Okay stop your daydreaming Rebecca, throw the sodding' rose.

"Bye Aunt Mae, I'll miss you," she said just loud enough to lift a few umbrellas.

But I won't miss you, will I? And why should I? After all it was Eliz-A-Beth who was given a brand-new Ferrari on Christmas day, not me! It even had a pretty pink bow tied around its shiny red bonnet. Spoilt bitch! But don't worry, Aunt

Mae didn't forget me. Oh no, Christmas was always so special to her. She bought me a dirty stinking puppy, and within an hour of this… this thing trotting up the path, it had crapped all over the Axminster carpet in the hall. Take a wild guess who had to clear that up. Yes, me! I mean, who am I? I'm just the carer. But it doesn't matter now, does it? The puppy's long gone. I've seen to that. Oh! How Eliz-A-Beth screamed as its tiny little bones were trapped and crushed under the wheels of her brand-new Ferrari that Christmas night. She ran into the house crying and screeching like a mad woman, and wouldn't come out until Mikey, that pompous prick of a husband of hers, had washed all the red clotty blood off the front tyre and scraped its stringy brains off the bright yellow brake callipers. It didn't actually occur to her for one tiny minute did it? That the puppy was already dead!

You see it was me all along. I poisoned the animal. I mean they don't perform post-mortems on puppies, do they? So, here I am standing at the graveside, shedding fountains of tears, crying the cry of the wise, just like the professional mourner I've become.

Occasionally I offer a loud howling sob followed up with a light pat of the eyes, only to be outdone by that daughter of hers, that bitch Eliz-A-Beth stood opposite responding with a loud and glorified wail of her own. But, of course, hers is way louder.

God, she's so gooood that one! But, rest assured, I'm so much better. Eliz-A-Beth threw a single red rose onto the coffin. *Copycat! Ought to be on the stage that one. Wish I had a camera. Oh well lookee here Mikey, Elizabeth's loving, caring husband is staring at me. I think he wants me again. Don't you even think about it Mikey. I mean she won't be thrilled, will she? Not when she finds out about us. Oh, bless them. Look, they've linked arms. How sweet. Oh, Eliz-A-Beth you sad, naïve little bitch, can't you see him staring at my thighs. I'm pouting again, puffing out my cherry lips. I love this game.*

Who's that stranger over there? Why does he keep looking at me? He's all on his own holding an umbrella. I've never seen him before. It's not like he's doing anything odd, it's just that every time I glance over his eyes want to mirror mine. What does he want? He's pulled the umbrella over his face now. Weirdo! I mean, I'm beautiful I know, but stop staring will you! None of it matters a hoot though does it? I'm so looking forward to the reading on Wednesday...

2.The Reading

"Thank you for coming in today ladies. Please do take a seat," said Dominic Symes, Senior Partner of Montague Symes & Co family solicitors, representing Eliz-A-Beth Baker.

"Thank you, Mr Symes, but before I sit down will you answer me a simple question?" replied an over-anxious Eliz-A-Beth."

"Yes, Mrs Baker, feel free, ask away," said Symes sitting himself down in his winged-backed leather chair looking particularly hot and beginning to quiver nervously.

"Well Mr Symes, if I may be so bold?" said Eliz-A-Beth, who was clearly in a tizzy. "What on earth is this awful woman doing here? She has nothing to do with my family! As you know my dear brother passed away years ago, and I am the sole heir to my mother's estate."

Eliz-A-Beth sat down in her chair crossing her legs before turning her venomous outburst towards Rebecca. "Go on then Rebecca tell me, enlighten us all why don't you?" she declared. "What the hell are you doing here?"

Time for a bit of play acting, I like that, thought Rebecca, searching her handbag for a tissue she knew wasn't there.

"I am here today Eliz-A-Beth because dear Aunt Mae invited me here! Apparently, I have been left something in her will. Can you pass me a tissue Mr Symes please? Oh God, I miss her so much, so much."

I deserve a bloody Oscar for that one.

"Of course, Miss Thorneycroft," said Symes passing her the box on his desk, watching as Eliz-A-Beth rocked backwards and forwards in her chair, before once more focusing her unwanted attention on the poor, and by now highly emotional, solicitor.

"Well, it's quite beyond me why a woman like this, a bloody carer of all people, an uneducated low life should be left anything at all! Mummy only employed her because she felt sorry for the stupid bitch! She only worked for her for two soddin years! Okay you might think I'm overreacting here, but come on tell me what she is doing here?"

Symes, sat with his elbows resting on the desk and hands forming the shape of a cathedral, leant forward and wondered if he was sat on the other side of the desk would he be asking the same question himself.

"Well Mrs Baker," he replied. "Despite how you may feel about all of this, it is my legal duty as your family solicitor to remind you that your mother's Last Will and Testament was, and still is, legally binding. You see, your mother came in to see me a couple of weeks before she passed away and was very explicit and detailed in her instructions. Miss Thorneycroft here was not party to that meeting, she was asked to wait for your mother outside in the secretary's office. So, there can be no question of coercion or duress. Your mother's decision was reached quite independently."

Symes sat back in his chair as Eliz-A-Beth held her hand to her mouth attempting to understand that not only had her mother neglected to inform her of the meeting, she hadn't invited her to attend either! She sat in complete shock, looking across at a perfectly calm Rebecca who was busily picking away at her manicured red nails.

Bizarrely, the whole thing reminded Rebecca of a scene from a *Rocky* film – the one where two bloodied old boxers faced each other across a filthy canvas, both square on points but still slugging it out for a knockout in the final round.

So, go on Eliz-a-Beth! she thought, *let it all out, reveal yourself you bitch! But no, you won't, will you? Because you're not ready yet, are you?*

"Well Mr Symes, if that's the case then I suppose it's time we moved on. Let's all hear for ourselves what this dreadful woman has managed to swindle out of my dear mummy."

Stay calm Rebecca, you've won! Deal with her later.

"Okay Mrs Baker, and Miss Thorneycroft if that clears things up, then we'll start the reading, shall we?"

"Please do Mr Symes, this should be entertaining," Elizabeth venomously chirped as Symes looked over his gold-rimmed spectacles at the large official-looking file he was grasping in his hands. Coughing pompously, he began.

"Montague Symes & Co have been appointed sole executors of the last Will and Testament for the late Mrs Mae Victoria Josephine Wilson, and the document I am holding here in my hand is the amended version dated 12 March 2015. This replaces the previous version dated 23 June 2012, your late mother signed in this office. The sum of all cash monies held in perpetuity by Montague Symes & Co on behalf of your late mother amount to…"

Symes then paused for effect as he pressed the centre of his round spectacles further up his nose and pretended to search the paperwork.

"Let me see now? Yes, here it is. The figure is four hundred and thirty-seven thousand, eight hundred and fifty-nine pounds, and eighty-one pence." Symes shared a steely glance between them both, allowing a momentary pause before once more returning his attention to the reading.

"These funds in their entirety have been left solely to you Mrs Baker."

Eliz-A-Beth clapped childishly then, realising she'd unwittingly exposed herself, quickly looked back down at the carpet. Symes continued… "Mrs Baker, your mother has also bequeathed you the Spanish villa in Javea, Alicante; the house here in Clifton Height's, Bristol and, of course, the Bentley Azure."

It's getting worse, hold on your turn is coming.

Symes held his hand to his mouth letting out a light cough as he flicked over to the next page.

"Now, turning to you Miss Thorneycroft. Mrs Wilson has left you nine thousand eight hundred shares that she held in various stocks and government bonds, the value as of midday today using our own online version of *stock watch*, amount to a little over one hundred and seventy-five thousand, two hundred and nineteen pounds, and eight pence."

"What! No way!" yelled Eliz-A-Beth across the desk, her face bright red in irritation and her fists tightly clenched. "I can't believe this is happening! I'll sue, I'll…"

"Please try and control yourself Mrs Baker!" said Symes attempting to assert some authority. "I do realise how upsetting this must be for you, but the law is the law and there is nothing you, or indeed I, can do about it."

Eliz-A-Beth glared at him across the desk with contempt and disgust and, feeling distraught, leant back in her chair.

Very cleverly, however, Symes had something up his sleeve, something he hoped might just be enough to placate the now thoroughly distressed, almost hysterical, Eliz-A-Beth. He offered her a sweetener.

"Of course, all the furniture, the paintings and the other personal items, including your mother's rare and expensive jewellery collection are left solely to you, Mrs Baker."

Symes smiled awkwardly across the desk, hoping beyond hope that Eliz-A-Beth would be satisfied with this.

She wasn't! Instead, she became angrier and angrier by the minute. So, once more pressing his spectacles to his face and realising his shot at mediation had failed, Symes quickly resumed the reading. Swallowing hard he continued…

"Before we conclude the reading here today, I am afraid there is the matter of our fees Mrs Baker," Symes remarked almost apologetically.

Knew he wouldn't forget that, thought Rebecca.

"They amount to… yes here we are… they amount to twenty-one thousand, two hundred- and eighteen-pounds including the VAT. There's nothing I can do about the dreaded VAT I'm afraid."

Symes smiled meekly across the desk at both of them before finally adding, "So, I am pleased to inform you that now concludes the reading here today," he added, clearing his throat, "Unless of course either of you two *'uh hum ladies'* have any further questions?"

"I don't," Rebecca meekly confirmed thinking: *not me Symes, keep the furniture, shame about the jewellery, but good old cash is king. Thank you, Aunt Mae.*

The small office was momentarily silent as Symes closed the large file with a dull *thud* and, almost as if he'd fired a shot from a starting pistol, Eliz-A-Beth instantly stood up and peered across the desk at him.

"You have to be fucking joking Symes!" she shouted at the top of her voice and pointing directly at Rebecca. "This evil little bitch here gets a hundred and seventy-five grand of my mother's fuckin' money. No way! I'll contest it! You are a fraud, Thorneycroft, and an evil robbing bitch!"

Unfortunately for the dear sweet Eliz-A-Beth, Rebecca had seen and heard enough and, despite previously assuring herself that she'd remain calm and aloof and ignore the rantings of what she considered to be a mad woman, her outburst was inevitable and arrived without warning.

"Oh, for fuck's sake sit down you stupid bitch!" Rebecca shouted standing over her. "And stop making such a bloody scene you spoilt little cow! Bit too late to moan about it now isn't it *Lizzie* love? Symes can't help you now, there's not a bloody thing he or you can do about it. I could kill for a fag right now. Are we done here Mr Symes?"

"Miss Thorneycroft! Mrs Baker! Symes pleaded, as he stood up. "I must say that this is not the time or the place to argue about this! Can you both try and conduct yourself in a reasonable manner. And Miss Thorneycroft will you please sit down!"

Symes pulled the bottom of his waistcoat down, puffing out his wrinkled cheeks and sat back down in his chair, recognising that his time representing the Wilson family's financial affairs was clearly at an end. But he didn't care. After all, the money Eliz-A-Beth had just inherited would all be gone in a couple of years. He'd bet a year's salary on that.

So, moving on nervously and cleaning his spectacles with his handkerchief, he returned his attention once more to the now seated Rebecca.

"The late Mrs Wilson asked me to hand deliver this envelope to you Miss Thorneycroft. It contains the original share certificates which, for a small fee, Montague Symes & Co will be happy to redeem for you. The money could be safely deposited in your account by say…"

Syme's squinted as he looked down at his watch, "… four o'clock this afternoon."

Smile take the envelope and calm down Rebecca. Two years of cleaning that shitty ass. Was it worth it? For a hundred and seventy-five grand it was. Of course, it was so on to the next one!

"Thank you, Mr Symes," Rebecca confirmed. "You have my bank details. If you could kindly arrange for the funds to be deposited in my account that would be greatly appreciated. This afternoon, by four o'clock you say Mr Symes?"

Her question was clearly designed to propel the now fuming Eliz-A-Beth into yet another frenzy. And as sure as eggs are eggs it did.

"Yes, that's what I just said Miss Thorneycroft," answered Symes, "By four o'clock this afternoon," he confirmed fully aware of the game Rebecca was now playing.

Time to leave, Rebecca. The fuse is lit.

"Goodbye Mr Symes. Oh, and bye, bye Eliz-A-Beth," Rebecca said fluttering her fingers as close to Eliz-A-Beth's face as she dared. "I've already packed my things, so there's no need for me to call round to the house or to ever speak to you ever again."

"So, goodbye Eliz-A-Beth, and to hell with you! Oh, damn! Silly me, I nearly forgot; I knew there was something else I wanted to share with you. Your Mikey really is a crap shag! I'd dump him if I were you. Believe me *Lizzy baby…* There's 'soooo' much better out there."

Eliz-A-Beth immediately stood up, lifted her leg, removed her black high heel shoe and threw it at Rebecca but, anticipating this reaction, she quickly ducked and it missed her head by less than an inch – instead embedding itself into Symes' framed solicitor's indentures, smashing them and the ornate wooden frame they were contained in to pieces.

Bit ironic that, thought Rebecca, smiling to herself.

Satisfied? No, actually ecstatic! Rebecca didn't say another word. She simply stood up, left the room, and closed the heavy mahogany door quietly behind her, as she strode confidently down the stuffy old Victorian hallway. She barely heard Eliz-A-Beth screaming at the hapless Symes in the background as she offered a satisfied smile towards the blonde secretary, sat at her desk busily painting her nails in the outer office.

Emerging into the full brightness of a winter's day opposite the imposing structure of Isambard Kingdom Brunel's Clifton Suspension Bridge, she tightened her belt on her fake Prada coat. The air outside was biting and fresh, the snow-covered scene with the beautiful Georgian mansions nestled in the background were simply beautiful.

The day was so full of life. Her life…

"Ding-dong," announced her arrival at the Bridge Café as she opened the door to her favourite coffee shop set in the most stylish part of Clifton Village.

"Small latte please Lucie. Oh, and I think I'll take one of those fresh cream cakes over there," Rebecca said pointing at the sweet selection. "Have you seen anything of Tom today Lucie?" she asked politely.

"No, sorry Rebecca, he hasn't been in this morning. Wasn't that awful news about your dear Aunt Mae, such a lovely old soul she was. I mean she passed away so quickly didn't she… She always looked so healthy."

"She wasn't my aunt Lucie! She was my employer!" Rebecca snapped back, immediately regretting the unintended outburst. "I'm sorry Lucie, I didn't mean to be rude, I'm just really upset, that's all."

"Don't you apologise to me Rebecca; I think I know more than anyone what dear Aunt Mae meant to you."

No, you don't you stupid bitch. "Thanks Lucie, yes she meant the world to me."

Rebecca sat down throwing her velvet black gloves onto the top of the round glass table staring out through the frost-covered Georgian windows at the brightly lit jewellery shops that criss-crossed Clifton's Princess Victoria Street, promising herself she'd take a peek later.

Snapping her from her daydreaming the door *dinged* and in walked Tom Thorneycroft brushing the fresh snow from his tatty old bomber jacket as he stamped his slush-covered feet onto the entrance mat.

"The usual Tom is it?" said the good-hearted Lucie pointing at the last Cornish pasty on the top shelf.

"God, you're on the ball today Lucie! Give a man a chance to get his coat off will you girl. But the answer is yes Lucie, and make sure it's not too hot this time," was Tom's curt reply as he rubbed his cold wrinkled hands together, taking a seat opposite Rebecca.

"So, how did we get on then Becks?" he asked pulling his chair closer to the table. "Come on spill the beans. What happened at the solicitors?"

Why does he always call me Becks? I hate it! Mum would turn in her bloody grave.

"Well not very good I'm afraid Tom," was Rebecca's satirical reply trying to keep a straight face.

Now who's playing who Tom? she asked herself sensing that awful temper of his bubbling away somewhere under the surface.

Tom totally ignored Lucie as she placed the latte and the overheated Cornish pasty down on top of the glass table as he sat there, arms folded, with his chair rocking backwards and forwards – the timed awkward movements normally a precursor to one of his violent ranting outbursts. But Rebecca was feeling rather brave and watched as his thin cruel lips curled downwards and his face gradually turned a lighter shade of scarlet; his pale green eyes matched hers across the table. And it was about then he finally snapped.

"The reading Becks!" he shouted banging his large fist down on the top of the glass table. "What happened at the fucking reading! Tell me or so help me, I'll…?"

"You'll do what?" Rebecca immediately cut in matching his glare across the table and sitting further forward in her chair. "Go on tell me. What do you think you can do to me that you haven't done already? Just fucking try it you rotten bastard!"

Rebecca was the one shouting now, and really didn't care if Lucie, or indeed anyone else in the café, heard as she slammed the empty coffee cup down on the table cracking the bone china saucer.

Almost instantly the place fell silent. Tom looked around the café where most of the patrons had stopped what they were doing, a few looked away. An elderly man started to rise from his chair, only to have his wife's arm tug him back into his seat. Tom shouted from his chair, "Mind your own fucking business," as humiliation, and its best friend embarrassment, cut through him like a knife through warm butter. You could hear a pin drop as the totally bewildered, shocked and thoroughly belittled Tom slumped back in his chair, with a look of resignation across his face, as he stared across at Rebecca who was still glaring at him defiantly.

Then, almost like a wolf who suddenly realised his prey refused to be dinner that night, he lowered his voice and was almost pleading with her, "Come on love be reasonable, will you? I've put a lot of hard work into this, don't forget it was me who nicked that bloody passport so I could get that job at Somerset house. It was me that dosed up Aunt Mae with all those bloody sedatives. So, cough up. Come on, tell your old *dad* what really happened?"

Tom was unashamedly begging her and wiped a dribble of frothy spittle from the corner of his thin lips, before repeating the question.

"Come on? Tell me. How did we really get on?"

"One hundred and seventy-five grand in cashed-in shares, that's how we *really* got on!" Rebecca stoically replied watching his reaction from across the table, as his small round spectacles glinted in the winter sunshine and the ex-con, murderer and blackmailer released a nasty smile as he took a greedy bite of his Cornish pasty.

"That's better, that's much better love," he said crunching through his reply. His whole attitude and persona changing faster than a rat scaling a drainpipe.

"We can do something with that love," he said wiping the side of his thin mouth with his tatty sleeve. "Tidy amount that,

usual arrangement is it, fifty-fifty? So, when do I see *my* cash?"
he asked, munching on the remnants of his pasty.

"Symes said it should clear the bank by about four this
afternoon, so I'll draw it out in the morning. I don't know what
you're getting so bloody excited about though because that's
nowhere near enough; I need three or four times that before I
can get out."

*I so want this to end, but I know getting out is the last thing
in his twisted mind. The bastard's craved hard cash his whole
life. Not just that, he wants payback for the seven years he
spent in Pentonville on a trumped-up charge of conspiracy and
fraud.*

*It doesn't bother him in the slightest, does it, that he should
have been serving a life sentence for murder? In his deranged
mind he's innocent of the fraud and deception charges, So, to
him the young lad's murder was completely irrelevant.*

Suddenly, Rebecca had this urge to just stand up and run, to
rid herself forever of this evil monster sat opposite her, to start
again somewhere else. She detested this man with every ounce
of her being. But she couldn't walk away because the time
wasn't right. She just wasn't ready. Not yet anyway. Rebecca

correctly predicted his next question and, as sure as eggs are eggs, he asked, "Did he touch you? That Mike I mean, did he hurt you in any way Becks? You can tell me."

Rebecca knew this morbid interest in her was more about satisfying his own sexual interest than any real care he had for her well-being... or safety.

"No, he didn't, and why would you care? Leave it alone will you. The deal's done and we're up, so let's get on with the next one. You got anything new for me?"

Tom was struggling to calm himself down and, as he wiped his greasy shaking hands on his knees, he answered, "Yeah, Becks. As it happens, I have," he said in an almost boastful tone.

Good, thought Rebecca, *because next time your cut's a third.*

Crossing his legs, Tom slid a tatty old piece of paper across the glass table towards her. She could sense his eyes looking her up and down, wishing she was ten or eleven again, so he could delve about her body without interruption.

Bastard!

"Well there are two to choose from this time Becks," Tom said, tapping the piece of paper. "The first one is an old girl called Enid Williams. I nicked her details from a file at work. The second is a bloke called Wilf. He's advertising for a carer with an agency called Grant's just down the road from here. You'll need to apply for the job with them. The choice is yours."

Typed in bold print:

Somerset House: File ID: 033228BA Williams:
Enid Josephine
D.O.B. 28:03: 1932
Address: Lonsdale House, Whittingham Crescent, Bath.
Known Dependants: None. Marital Status: Widow.

Somerset House: File ID: 0331338TA Kennedy:
Arthur Wilfred
D.O.B. 20:08: 1928
Address: Holmlea, 26 Royal Crescent, Sneyd Park, Bristol.
Known Dependants: None. Marital Status: Batchelor.

"This will be our third in four years," Tom said tapping the piece of paper again. "Time is ticking by, we need to get this one over and done with, no more hanging about. Get in there, get 'em signed up and *puff* off they go to the happy hunting ground."

Tom sat there, with his shoulders moving up and down chuckling to himself waiting for Rebecca to burst out laughing like he'd delivered the punch line of a really funny joke. But Rebecca wasn't laughing, instead she offered him nothing more than a steely glance by way of reply.

"You certainly do pick 'em don't you? Sneyd Park, Whittingham bloody Crescent. These two alone must be worth millions," Rebecca remarked as his eyes lit up like someone who'd just won the lottery.

He's not even my father. Oh no, he's just my stepfather, and I despise him. I must admit I do feel sorry for him in a bizarre sort of way, but that's just pity isn't it? You see, he was all I had at the time. My biological father was long gone by then, he'd left mum years before. I remember her telling me how she'd woken up one morning to find a "Dear Joan" pinned to the dressing table, telling her he'd buggered off to America. I can remember at the time not even knowing where America was.

Then, two years later bang and the cancer took mum, and I was left alone with this… this bastard. I tried to be a good girl, not to provoke him or bother him in any way. I'd sit for hours in my bedroom playing with my dolls as he entertained his so-called lady friends. The number of women I caught him with ran easily into treble figures, but he'd just laugh at me from the bed, half naked, roaring drunk and throw empty beer cans at me as I tried to clean the filthy flat or clear up his spliffs and empty the overflowing ashtrays.

But that's not the whole story. No, it's not even close. It was the abuse that pushed me over the edge. I can remember it like it happened yesterday. It would usually start with a strange look or a stare followed by an awkward touch, then he'd tell me what a good girl I was and how it was okay, because we weren't blood relatives and weren't breaking the law. And how I mustn't tell anyone. You see this bastard was all I had. Cold, evil bastard!

The Avon and Somerset social report said:

Mrs Eileen McWhirter
Bristol City Council Social Services
100 Temple Street
Bristol BS1

The matter was brought to my attention by a neighbour of the Thorneycroft's who reported the problem to me, and I quote from their statement.

"Young Rebecca is clearly underfed and is kept up to all hours by constant shouting and smashing of glasses from inside the flat. Mr Thorneycroft seems to have regular female visitors late at night, and Rebecca has been seen on several occasions walking the streets of Bristol smoking cigarettes looking totally lost and bedraggled."

The report went on to say:

"This is an extremely difficult and distressing environment for a young girl of this age and the council recommend that before any permanent physiological damage is done, a foster home or social care should be arranged at the earliest possible opportunity."

I'd read it four times. After that, I was pushed from pillar to post, from one foster home to another. Then I was simply packed off to what some well-meaning geek at the council referred to as a "safe house", filled to the brim with strangers. A few months later I was moved again to another childrens' home called Pendleton, somewhere down on the Dorset coast and it was there that I met Pauly. Pauly was... sorry correction (is) my best friend. You could argue that Pauly was my first love, and you'd be right because he was.

But shall we say Pauly had other interests in life and would shrug off my continual offers of sex with a laugh or a gentle shrug. Anyway, a couple of months after I arrived, I caught him in his room in a rather uncompromising position with one of what I used to term "inmates" and this particular inmate just happened to be a man.

So, any love I had for him was short lived but, Pauly being Pauly, he never gave up on me. Once, he even stopped one of the male staff from raping me by grabbing him around the back of the neck and pulling him off. Pauly is really big you see, even then when we were no older than fifteen and I was a blossoming young beauty, Pauly stood well over six feet five and was at least sixteen stone. Pauly is the kindest man I have ever met, a true gentle giant and as soon as this is all over, I'm heading his way. I must call him.

He lives in a town called Javea, somewhere in Spain, and runs a bar called Gee-Gee's with his husband Brett. As soon as this is done, I'm right there with you Pauly.

In the meantime, I think I'll pick Wilf. He's a bit older and probably won't be around as long. Anyway, I adore Sneyd Park...

3. Symes

As previously arranged, Rebecca arrived at the offices of Montague Symes & Co for her ten o'clock meeting with Dominic Symes and was cordially offered a seat in the reception by the same blonde nail-painting secretary she'd met the day before.

"May I have your name and the time of your appointment please," the secretary asked, faking a false upper-class accent.

"Thorneycroft... Miss Rebecca Thorneycroft and the appointment is for ten o'clock with Mr Symes," Rebecca curtly replied casting a discomforting glance back at her before she walked across the reception and sat down on one of the ornate Victorian chairs.

She could hear the secretary announcing her arrival on the internal phone. "A Miss Rebecca Thorneycroft is here to see you Mr Symes, would you like me to show her in? Yes, yes of course Mr Symes, that's fine, I'll let her know."

Replacing the phone, the secretary looked across the reception interrupting Rebecca's reading of *Tatler* as she verbally announced, "Mr Symes will see you now Miss

Thorneycroft, you're free to go in. I presume you know where his office is?"

"You presume right," was Rebecca's curt reply, using an equally false upper-class accent.

Dominic Symes' eyesight wasn't what it used to be. His thin lips, scrawny appearance and short stature reminded Rebecca of a modern-day *Ebenezer Scrooge*. But old Symes certainly knew the difference between thrift and opulence and under no circumstances could Symes ever be described as opulent.

The sign on the door told her to, "Knock before entering". But Rebecca chose to ignore that, turned the handle and walked straight in to find Symes staring out of his office window, his hands clasped firmly behind his back.

"Oh, do come in Rebecca, why don't you?" He greeted her, mockingly lifting an eyebrow.

"There's no need for formalities here is there Mr Symes? I think we've known each other far too long for that sort of bullshit. Don't you?"

Symes' response to Rebecca's comment was no more than a disgruntled huff, followed by a wave of his hand as he pointed his scrawny finger towards the chair opposite his large mahogany desk.

"Sit down Rebecca. This shouldn't take very long; I assume you've not come in empty handed?"

"Then you presume right Mr Symes," Rebecca replied, crossing her legs and sliding a large brown envelope across his highly polished desk.

"All there is it? I don't need to count it do I?" Symes enquired, as he nodded at the envelope.

"Count it if you want, it's all there, twenty-five grand in used fifties, not a penny more, not a penny less."

The corners of his thin mouth offered nothing more than a greedy smile as he fingered the large brown envelope and stuffed it into the top drawer of his desk.

"So, on to the next one then is it?" he asked, wrongly assuming his question was rhetorical. "You and that father of yours must have another *victim* in the pipeline," he added, emphasising the word victim.

Rebecca hated Symes! His nonchalant: *Nobody can touch me* attitude really pissed her off. She snarled back at his intimation that Tom Thorneycroft was her biological father.

"Let's get something straight here shall we Symes," she said leaning across the desk, causing him to retreat further into his winged-back chair. "Number one! Tom bloody Thorneycroft is not my father, as well you know! Number two! You just stick to your side of the bargain forging these wills, and I'll stick to mine. Okay! Otherwise you might just find yourself on the receiving end of a visit from my *father* as you're so fond of calling him. And it's my guess you wouldn't like that, now would you Symes?"

Symes sat bolt upright in his chair, clearly shocked at her outburst, a mixture of fear and loathing crossed his gaunt looking features as he struggled to control his bladder.

"I never respond to threats Rebecca," he stated feigning a little courage. "But due to the… shall we say sensitive nature of our little *business arrangement*, I will ignore that last comment of yours. Now, if that is all, I have another client waiting to see me."

"Yes," Rebecca confirmed asserting control. "That will be all for now Symes and I'll be sure to pass your best wishes on to Tom. So, until the next time, bye."

Rebecca rose from the chair and strode confidently across the room as the terrified solicitor pretended to tidy the papers on his desk. Rebecca hoped that *next time* there would be no need to involve a moron like him.

But she knew that whatever happened, there just had to be a next time…

4. Wilf

Wilf likes to be called just that, *Wilf.* He was born *Artur Benjamin Goldstein* and he was Jewish. Wilf is a Holocaust survivor, orphaned when his parents were murdered the night of *Kristallnacht* when thousands of Jews across Berlin were rounded up, killed or sent to one of the *Konzentration Lagers* rapidly springing up across Adolf Hitler's thousand-year Reich.

Wilf was one of the lucky ones. He arrived in Harwich, England late one freezing night in 1938, alone, penniless, parentless and stateless. He was one of the ten thousand children granted permission to leave Nazi Germany under the so-called *Kinder Transport*, so generously allowed by the then Reichsführer of the Schutzstaffel (head of the SS), Heinrich Himmler himself.

Two nights before *Kristallnacht,* Wilf's wealthy parents packed his bags and insisted that, whatever happened to him and no matter where he ended up, he was to keep his coat with him at all times. They'd told him it represented his freedom, a ticket to a better life and that he must only look inside the lining when he was quite alone.

Adopted a year later by a distant cousin of the famous *Kennedy* family of Martha's Vineyard, Massachusetts, Wilf was sent off to boarding school, where his conversion to Catholicism took less than two terms and his broad Berlin accent was non-existent in three.

Sat in his winged-back chair enjoying the warmth of the sun shining through his picturesque Tudor window, Wilf was doing what he always did on a Saturday morning – reading his diary. The same diary he'd so religiously kept up to date prior to his arrival on English shores, back in 1938.

"Ding dong."

Wilf looked up from his chair towards the hallway. He disliked interruptions and was exhausted by continuously interviewing carers. Only a month had passed since his last carer had resigned without notice. She'd been his seventh in as many months. Wilf quickly locked away his diary in the top drawer of his desk using the key he carefully guarded on a chain around his neck.

"Ding dong."

"I'm coming, I'm coming," he shouted from the hall, shuffling off towards the door, irritated that these so-called carers thought it prudent, even advantageous to always arrive at least ten minutes early.

"Hold on to your bloody horses, early or not, if you aren't right, you aren't right," he muttered to himself as he opened the door. He was immediately captivated by the sight of a stunning woman who'd arrived with the morning sunshine, spreading its rays behind a beautiful face wrapped in a brown fur hat pulled down so perfectly and eloquently revealing only the lobes of her delicate feminine ears. For a moment Wilf was speechless, admiring this wondrous vision that had somehow appeared at his door. He marvelled at her womanly curves so very perfectly wrapped up, almost like a Christmas present, stood before him in a long coat, wondering if this could be the new carer.

Pulling his arched back upright and attempting to regain some small level of masculinity and a semblance of self-respect, he asked, "Can... can... I help you?" Immediately regretting his stuttered request.

"Yes, thank you. I'm here for the interview, Grant's the agency sent me over, I hope I'm not too early. You must be Wilf... my name is Rebecca, that is Rebecca Thorneycroft."

39

Wilf stood silent and open mouthed, holding the door open and nervously shifting his weight from one foot to the other. Acutely aware of the fact that he'd not washed, shaved or dressed, he regretted greeting this woman in his grubby pyjamas and house coat caught like a rabbit in headlights.

Regaining some composure, he felt extremely awkward and vulnerable. Wilf took two steps back and invited her in.

"Please come in. I'm very sorry, I wasn't expecting you so early, I've…"

"Entirely my fault Wilf," Rebecca interjected holding out her soft white hand, "I hope you don't mind me calling you Wilf, do you?" she said pouting those cherry red lips of hers.

"No, not at all, please, please do come in," Wilf replied, enjoying the soft touch of her young hand. "My office is just down the hall, third door on the left. Please go in and make yourself comfortable. I'll only be a few minutes; I need to run off and change."

"Thank you, Wilf." Rebecca gently unbuttoned her coat, revealing a stunning floral dress, as she purposely brushed against his nervous frame and entered the grand hallway, her jet-black hair flowing from side to side.

She could feel his beady eyes burning into her taught backside as she slowly and provocatively strolled down the long hallway, hesitating now and then to admire the grand old paintings and mahogany cabinets overflowing with silver and gold artefacts.

"Just give me ten minutes Rebecca and I'll be right with you," said Wilf shuffling off towards the stairs.

"Take your time Wilf," was Rebecca's calm reply as she mused: *Got you Wilf, keep looking, you're all mine now.*

Entering the office and making herself comfortable in the leather chair opposite Wilf's imposing mahogany desk, with the sunlight still glinting its rays through the open stained-glass window, she noticed that an aroma of expensive Havana cigars filled the room. She didn't mind that. After all, wasn't that the smell of money… real money.

That desk alone must be worth thousands, she thought, enjoying the silence, admiring the blatant opulence that bordered on vulgarity and revelling in the wealth exhibited around her. *I so want this*, she mused as she took in her surroundings.

Fifteen minutes later and with the hem of her dress tucked purposely above her right knee, Wilf entered the office and shuffled over to his desk looking rather splendid in his navy-blue sports jacket with gold buttons, and claret cravat.

Rebecca thought she could smell *Old Spice* aftershave as he wafted passed her chair like a young toddler or clearly a man on a mission.

"Well Rebecca, it's very nice to meet you," he said making himself comfortable in his huge leather chair. "I must admit that you are the youngest of the candidates I've interviewed so far. Please tell me about yourself… what experience do you have?"

Rebecca watched as his eyes travelled from one part of her body to another. To her, Wilf was like an older, much richer and posher version of her stepfather, Tom Thorneycroft. *Just another dirty old git*, she thought.

She noticed a silver chain around his neck entangled in his silk cravat, the same one he was wearing when he'd answered the front door only fifteen minutes earlier. *What the hell's the chain for then?* she wondered as she cleverly responded to his question.

"Well, before she passed away my last employer, a Mrs Mae Wilson, very kindly provided me with an excellent reference. It's right here in my handbag."

Rebecca bent forwards allowing the front of her dress to drape slightly open, just enough to reveal a glimpse of her lovely white breasts with their large brown nipples. Wilf felt his heartbeat go into overdrive as fifteen years of unwanted celibacy stirred in his loins.

Handing him the reference, he took a hurried look at the scrawled handwritten letter without really taking it in, attempting to clear his mind of that wondrous nipple. He wished he could touch it. Maybe even lick it. Just the once.

Stop! his mind screamed. *Stop it now you dirty old man. She's young enough to be your granddaughter.*

But he couldn't. Wilf was very ill, and always had been. His last carer had recognised this, and it was the reason she'd left him in such a hurry one night, leaving him drunk as he pleaded with her to come to his bed.

Wilf tried to gather his thoughts and continue the interview, which lasted about another hour. Rebecca treated him to a last lingering glimpse of that wonderous nipple of hers as she leant forward returning the reference to her handbag.

Feeling extremely hot, Wilf loosened his cravat and became aware that his chain was on show and quickly stuffed it back in his shirt, just as Rebecca looked up.

So, it's that important then, thought Rebecca.

"There is one other thing I need to mention before making my decision Rebecca," Wilf arrogantly announced, correctly assuming she would jump at the chance of his employ.

"It's an extremely important matter so please listen very carefully. I have a severe allergy and under no circumstances can nuts to be brought into the house. I hope that's clear!"

"Yes Wilf, perfectly clear," Rebecca replied, a little taken back by his instant transformation from kindly, although dirty, old man to spitting male diva. So, deliberately stumbling

through her response to place him off guard, she said, "Oh…
uh… yes, yes, of course Wilf, I totally understand…"

The stuttering was obviously for effect because Rebecca
wasn't at all fazed by such a pathetic outburst. In a way she felt
as though she was involved in some sort of outdated sitcom
and found it quite comical.

But Wilf, far from finished, raised his hand and interrupted
her mid-sentence. "That does, of course, include all other food
products containing even the slightest trace of nuts. Do you
like curry Rebecca?" Wilf asked, completely out of the blue.

"Yes, I love curry but…"

Before she could finish, Wilf once again cut her short.
"Good. Although I adore a nice curry Rebecca, nearly all of
them contain nuts so no curries are to be brought into the house
– is that clear?"

Wilf paused his verbal onslaught for a second, annoyingly
rocking back and forth in his chair, slamming his eyes for
effect… before finally adding.

"That is, apart from the curries that are specially prepared
for me by my good friend *Abdul* at the *Aziz Tandoori* on the

corner of Fairview Heights. Abdul is an old family friend and is fully aware of my allergy."

"Of course, Wilf," replied Rebecca humbly repeating Wilf's previous warning almost word for word. "Yes, I've got that, nothing containing nuts, and only curries from your friend Abdul at the Aziz Tandoori on Fairview Heights."

Rebecca faked a gentle pout, exaggerating a modest sulk as a child might who had been wrongly accused of stealing sweets. And almost instantly Wilf's face dropped to the floor.

"Oh Rebecca, I'm so sorry, I've upset you! I have to emphasise the importance as just a hint of a nut can bring on an anaphylactic shock. At eighty-seven and with a dicky heart, I have to be extremely careful."

It's worked, he's fallen for it.

Wilf chuckled to himself nervously, his eyes twinkled but Rebecca didn't laugh.

It's not my place to laugh at you is it Wilf? After all, you're my prospective employer so I'm supposed to respect you. The mere mention of you passing away would naturally upset me. Give me three months and you'll be gone, three months, that's all you have left. Aunt Mae took nearly two years. So, you should be a synch... nut allergy... weak heart... take your pick Rebecca.

Then completely out of the blue Wilf leant forward across the desk and said.

"Okay Rebecca, I've made my decision. I am going to offer you the position. How soon would you be able to start? I'm afraid you've found me in bit of a mess. I've been without a carer for a while now and things have started to, shall we say, mount up. Would you like to see your room? It's right next to mine on the first floor. I'm sure you'll find it more than adequate; it boasts its own en-suite bathroom and separate dressing room."

Got you Wilf... come to Rebecca. "No that won't be necessary Wilf," Rebecca replied calmly. "I'm in rather a hurry today I'm afraid. Would tomorrow afternoon be okay? I need to pack my things and organise some transport."

"I can always send my driver round to collect you if that would help?" Wilf said, trying hard to conceal his thoughts of what sort of *things* Rebecca might be referring to.

"No, no that's quite all right, I can take care of it, would around three be convenient for you Wilf?"

"Three's fine with me," Wilf replied, pulling a face like an excited child and wondering if that gave him enough time to install the camera in her room…

The following day Rebecca was dropped off, by Tom in his beaten-up old Ford Granada, one street away from Wilf's house and she knocked on the door a little after three o'clock. This time she couldn't hear any muttering or sounds of any kind as the door quickly swung open, and Wilf stood in the doorway looking not to dissimilar to an older version of *Robert de Niro* as he beckoned her in.

"Welcome, welcome Rebecca, come in, come in," he greeted. "Let me take those," Wilf said, pointing at the two bulging suitcases by her feet.

"No Wilf, that's quite all right, they're not heavy, I can manage. But thank you anyway," Rebecca replied politely, performing a half curtsy and offering him a provocative smile as she stepped across the threshold.

"This way Rebecca, your room is ready for you, it's just up here, follow me." Wilf toddled off ahead to lead the way as Rebecca struggled with the weight of the two heavy suitcases, watching in amazement as the eighty-seven-year-old literally romped up the stairs.

Amazing, hope he's not on bloody Viagra, thought Rebecca as she puffed and panted up the stairs before walking along the landing.

Entering the room, the lovely fragrance of potpourri, mixed with expensive French furniture polish and starched linen, immediately enveloped her. The bed was immaculately made with a quilted pink eiderdown covering its enormous expanse. Below that lay freshly ironed starched white cotton sheets neatly folded down both sides. The sash window facing the rear garden was surrounded by floral curtains that hung so eloquently and perfectly divided by great folds, brushing the thick gold carpet below.

The day's sunshine was filtering through the sash window. The room was perfect, and Rebecca was dumbstruck. Every nerve and every sense in her body tingled with excitement notifying her that she'd successfully arrived and that this was how life was meant to be. Not the one Tom Thorneycroft had so dispassionately thrust upon her.

Wilf politely offered his apologies saying he had to go and attend to some paperwork in his bedroom. Rebecca thanked him and said she was going to unpack then take a bath, if that was all right with him. And she would be down in a little while.

On hearing that, an excited Wilf thanked her then quickly scurried off to his bedroom to sort out his paperwork.

And turn the camera on next door…

5. McDermott

Detective Sergeant Andy McDermott was a serving police officer in the Avon and Somerset Constabulary and had been for nearly twenty-five years. In all that time, and on four separate occasions, he'd been passed over for promotion. This really pissed him off, but the remarks scribbled at the bottom of his last application were the ones that riled him the most.

"Just not a team player," it said. Adding "He lacks drive, stamina and ambition somehow."

The scrawny handwritten comments were those of Detective Superintendent Peter Goodfield, his immediate boss.

Rumour was rife and spreading like wildfire amongst his colleagues that McDermott was a womanising, bribe-able alcoholic. And the rumours were well founded because they were true. But things hadn't always been that way. Back in the summer of 1990, just like all the other new recruits he'd embarked on his career with nothing but promise and good intentions, finishing a very respectable second from a class of thirty at the police training college.

He was from a good family; his estranged father was an ex-copper and a damn good one at that. So, what had gone so horribly wrong? After all, he seemed to have it all going for him, didn't he? Anyone who knew him would agree that only a successful rewarding career lay ahead.

But somewhere deep down inside that *graveyard of all ambition*, that twisted master of minds *boredom and greed* had burrowed deep into McDermott's psyche. And inevitably only disenchantment and disillusionment followed.

Now aged 45, still moderately handsome but two stone overweight, he was looking forward to nothing more than a good old copper's pension following his recent divorce from his wife Penny. After all, he'd put the time in, hadn't he? But he'd given up chasing the donkey's tail years ago and that was why unsolved case files littered his untidy desk and he happily spent more time puffing on one of his favourite *Gitanes* in the station's smoking shelter or taking a quick gulp from his hip flask than rummaging through dusty old mug-shots of long-lost felons.

However, his boss, the superbly structured and fastidious Detective Superintendent Peter Goodfield, was a career copper and only last week had added yet another case file to the top of his huge pile. Its plain grey wallet sat precariously on top of the others threatening to fall to the dust ridden floor, given even the slightest hint of movement.

The case file, stamped with the usual "Avon and Somerset Constabularies" black and white logo, had a photograph of the suspect stapled to the front, with their name and unique eight-digit case number written in black felt tip, just below.

Somewhat invitingly, Rebecca Thorneycroft's colour photograph stared back at him, and McDermott wished that this stunning beauty, this vision of delight was right there in his office and astride his desk.

What a cracking looking bird, I wonder if she clocked me at the funeral? Who cares, I'd tail her anytime. I'd bet a month's pay she's a fucking demon in bed. Peter bloody perfect upstairs can go fuck himself, this beauty's all mine.

He started to read Rebecca's file for the fourth time:

Name: Thorneycroft, Rebecca Susan
Gender: Female
D.O.B. 21.06.1990
Marital Status: Single

Dependants: None

Last known address: Flat Four, Chatham House, Coldharbour Road, Redland, Bristol BS6 5A

Occupation: Full time social companion and carer for the elderly.

Notes: Suspect's stepfather is a Thomas Michael Thorneycroft, a career criminal, known throughout seven constabularies in the United Kingdom and Northern Ireland. Thomas Thorneycroft is currently on license and residing in the Bristol area after being convicted at Bristol Crown Court on 8 May 2012 on seven charges of fraud, and one further charge of deception. Sentencing Thorneycroft to a period of seven years, circuit Judge *Peter Llewellyn Jones* described him in his summing up as a "Career criminal, and a modern-day Fagin, who prayed on the elderly, the infirm and the most vulnerable in our society."

McDermott turned the page and was looking down at the twisted haggard lines covering every inch of Tom Thorneycroft's gaunt looking features. His list of previous offences ran to an extra four extra pages at the back of the thick file and inside, stapled to the cover, was a letter from DS Peter Goodfield he'd penned shortly before placing the file on McDermott's desk:

Andy,

<u>Rebecca Thorneycroft</u>

Now this might not come to anything and is probably just a whinging relative blowing off hot air but take a look anyway.

A Mrs Elizabeth Baker called into Redland nick yesterday and said she wanted to file a complaint. DS Mandy Smith was on duty at the time, so she took down her statement and, if you care to read it, this Mrs Baker seems to think that Rebecca Thorneycroft has been extorting money from elderly people. In this case, her mother.

DS Smith said she seemed to be a bit vague on how exactly this Thorneycroft woman was managing to do it. So, I checked out the last will and testament of Mrs Baker's mother, a Mrs Mae Wilson.

It says she left Thorneycroft a hundred and seventy-five grand in shares. Well, according to her solicitor, a brief by the name of Dominic Symes in Bristol who dealt with the will, it was all carried out quite legal and above board.

To me, it all looks a bit "Johnny Upright", but make sure you check her out anyway.

Put a tail on her and try and find out what she's up to, but don't spend too many hours on it. Don't forget, it's me that signs off the overtime.

Peter

P.S (the old man seems a bad lot).

McDermott flicked through Tom's lengthy charge sheet, it went and on for pages.

A bad lot? You are having a tin bath! Bad lot! He's a lot worse than that. You really are a pompous prick Goodfield.

6. Wilf

Rebecca was up bright and early on her first day and found a list of instructions had been pushed under her door. The scrawled handwriting read:

Dearest Rebecca,

Welcome to Holmlea.

Because of the size of the house I thought it might be better if I made a list of the daily chores (for want of a better word) that need attending to on a daily basis here at Holmlea.

The list went on and on, seven whole pages of unintelligible scribbling broken down into seven daily routines of cleaning, washing and cooking. All clearly designed to make sure the recipient had little or no time for themselves for the simple things in life such as eating, showering or even having a shit.

Wilf had written instructions for every day with the exception of Tuesdays and Sundays. Tuesdays Wilf would attend his bridge club in Hotwells so that was Rebecca's midweek day off. Sundays were a little different – as long as she'd prepared his roast dinner the night before she was allowed that day off as well.

Finally, under no circumstances whatsoever was she ever to enter his room without first being invited and she should always knock and then wait for an answer. He'd added as a sort of postscript that he, and he alone, would take care of cleaning his own room.

Rebecca's first day had started with the delivery of a full English breakfast and a pot of Earl Grey tea accompanied by three loud knocks on Wilf's door at the stroke of eight.

In between breakfast and lunch, she was expected to clear out five of the six fireplaces and fill up the coal scuttles. Then came the dusting, polishing and vacuuming of three huge sitting rooms. She then finally had to clean Wilf's office.

As she was polishing the top of his large mahogany desk, Rebecca sensed a movement behind her. Startled, she looked around to find Wilf dressed in his housecoat just two feet from where she was working.

"Sorry Rebecca I didn't mean to startle you," he said almost apologetically. "I thought I heard a noise, so I came in to investigate. I must say that was a wonderful breakfast you cooked this morning; you're quite the little housewife aren't you."

"Thank you, Wilf, my pleasure," said Rebecca, a little unnerved by his presence, especially since his housecoat draped slightly open below the waist and, from where she was standing, Wilf was clearly more pleased to see her, than her him.

An awkward silence ensued as Wilf's gaze matched hers as he looked her up and down and his eyes lustfully travelled her frame.

"Well Rebecca I think I'll take a bath," he suddenly declared scratching his chest and yawning. "If anyone calls or telephones please tell them I'm indisposed at the moment. Take a message and tell them I'll call back later."

"Okay, Wilf leave it to me; I've got five minutes left in here then I'll start lunch. Enjoy your bath."

"Thank you, Rebecca, toodaloo for noo," Wilf gleefully announced as he trotted off towards the stairs.

Rebecca waited for a moment quietly listening for the last of his footfalls from the landing above, then the *clunking* sound of the upstairs bathroom door being closed, the sound echoing down the stairs.

"Right, let's take a look in this desk of yours shall we Wilf?" she whispered, opening each one of the three drawers set either side of the huge desk. Unfortunately, inside was a disappointing mixture of old pens, discoloured photographs, rubbish and a few broken staplers scattered here and there. Apart from the last drawer which was locked. She yanked on the handle in frustration and unsurprisingly it didn't budge.

She knelt down to look underneath and could see four large triangular hand-made wooden brackets attached to each corner of the desk that connected the top to the drawers. She wondered if the desk might have been refurbished recently as the four screws securing the brackets to the frame were silver headed and neatly countersunk. Rebecca pulled herself up and rested her hand on the mahogany top deep in thought for a moment.

Today is Monday, so he'll be out at the bridge club all day tomorrow. So that's when I'll whip the top off and have a look for myself.

The next morning, following exactly the same routine, she delivered his breakfast accompanied by three loud knocks on his door then scurried off to iron his best white *Hugo Boss* shirt. The one he always wore when he was playing bridge.

An hour later, Wilf descended the stairs immaculately turned out in the freshly ironed shirt, a gold cravat, his black *Gucci* braces and pressed black trousers. Rebecca gracefully opened the front door and wished him a "very good day". On the other side of the gravel driveway was a chauffeur dressed in a jet-black uniform holding the rear door open on Wilf's silver on black *Rolls Royce Phantom.*

"See you later Rebecca, enjoy your day off and don't wait up for me, I'm usually a bit tiddly when I get home, especially after a few brandies," Wilf cheerfully announced as he whisked past acknowledging her with a smile, and a simple tap of his black felt fedora.

Rebecca watched him trundle across the driveway towards his waiting car and wondered to herself, *how long would it take to get the bloody top off?*

"Bye Wilf enjoy your day, byeee, see you later," she shouted waving like a long-lost friend as the electric gates slowly opened, and the huge beast pulled out onto the main road, leaving in its wake a trail of dust, gravel and bluey-white exhaust fumes.

"Right to the parlour. I need a toolkit," she said to herself slamming the front door.

Moments later, she reappeared armed with a large screwdriver, a claw hammer and a can of Pledge spray polish. She immediately got to work as one by one the screws creaked and moaned their way free. Each one seeming a little tighter than the last as they dropped to the floral carpet below.

Ten minutes later and covered in sweat she started to heave the desktop across when suddenly she heard the front doorbell being rung. Quickly pushing the desktop back into place, she walked across to the office door and looked down the hall. Standing the other side of the stained-glass window she could see an outline and this outline appeared to be wearing a hat not too dissimilar to a policeman's hat.

Gently, she closed the office door behind her and straightening her hair she took a deep breath and walked towards the front door.

"Who is it please," she asked through the glass. "Mr Kennedy isn't expecting any visitors today."

There was a short pause before the outline with the hat looked up and replied. "It's only me, it's Jack the postie, I've got a parcel for Wilf and it needs signing for I'm afraid."

"Oh, sorry Jack, I'll let you in," Rebecca anxiously replied, relieved that the hat didn't contain a policeman's head as she turned the large brass doorknob, and gingerly opened the front door.

"Sign here will you please Ma'am," said Jack offering her his portable script machine and a small brown box.

"It's a mobile phone I think," he added noticing her hands were trembling as she signed.

"Is there anything wrong Ma'am," Jack enquired, "You look a bit flustered," he said returning the machine back into his post office satchel.

"No, no I'm quite all right, I've been vacuuming all morning. I'm just feeling a little hot that's all. I'm fine but thank you for your concern. Oh, by the way Jack can I ask how you got in through the electric gates?"

Jack just there stood in the doorway open mouthed, his mind elsewhere wondering how a stripy old git like Wilf Kennedy had managed to land a beauty like this, wishing she'd invite him in for a morning coffee like Wilf always did. But Jack being Jack was far too shy to ask and anyway he was behind on his round. Suddenly remembering Rebecca's question, Jack blushed wondering if she'd noticed him staring at her breasts.

"Well, Wilf let me have the code because his legs aren't quite what they used to be. Anyway, really nice to meet you miss… uh?" he tentatively enquired.

"Thorneycroft, Miss Rebecca Thorneycroft," she replied wishing that this irritating little man standing between her finding out what was in that bloody desk would just piss off and get on with his round.

"Well bye for now Miss Thorneycroft," said Jack, politely tapping his peaked cap like a guard's officer might, "Hope we meet again sometime."

"Yes, thank you, and bye Jack," said Rebecca, slowly closing the front door and providing a fake blushful smile, more relieved than anything that the moron had finally departed.

Meet again? she thought. *A bloody postie, you can kiss my sweaty ass Jack. Get in the bloody queue.*

Rebecca stood leaning against the door for a moment, her chest heaving up and down concerned about the time. *It's twelve o'clock already. This has to be done today! Come on Rebecca. Get on with it.*

Back inside the office, she placed the claw hammer and the flat headed screwdriver back down on the carpet then, using her head as a lever, she pushed the desktop up and felt it slide sideways separating itself from the drawers with a loud *clunk*. Then, standing up and using every ounce of her strength, she started to slide the desktop forward, inch by inch, creaking as it moved. Careful not to overbalance and making sure she didn't topple it over, eventually the contents inside the top drawer revealed themselves and tucked neatly away inside was a small leather-bound book with the single word "Tagebuch" *(Diary)* imprinted on its front cover with a silver Nazi swastika and an eagle just below it. Rebecca, still balancing the weight of the desktop on top of the wooden frame picked up the book.

Wiping a bead of sweat from her face she opened the diary, turned to the first page and started to read. The handwriting was awful, scratched across the tatty yellowing paper like a doctor's prescription. But even worse, it was written in German so not one word, not one sentence made any sense to her. The dates were easy, that part was obvious *Octubre* clearly meant October. And 1938 meant just that, 1938. But the rest was just pure gibberish as far as she was concerned.

Pulling her iPhone 6S out from her pocket she pressed the camera icon, then one by one she started to laboriously photograph each page. There were eleven pages in total and it took nearly twenty minutes to photograph them all. When she'd finished, she placed the book carefully back in exactly the same position she'd found it, then gently and slowly slid the desktop across being extremely careful not to scratch or damage it in any way.

The process of reassembling the desk took her another sweat laden hour, as a few of the screws didn't quite line up and, on several occasions, she found herself heaving and pushing it a millimetre here and there, until finally she was done. She sprayed the desktop with furniture polish, carefully wiping away any traces of fingerprints from the top and bottom of the desk.

She'd read something recently about a free *google app* that, once the documents are pasted into the phone, automatically translates them into a language of choice. She sat down on the edge of the bed watching as the little blue download icon of the google app gradually filled up the screen and a message told her she was good to go. She pasted the first photograph and watched as Wilf's scrawny hand-written words were translated into English.

The first diary entry read:

29 October 1938, Berlin

I am left in my bedroom and can hear the sounds of gunfire outside. Papa is trying to comfort mama downstairs. The servants have all left saying they won't work for us filthy Jews any longer. Papa and mama are very scared, but they reassure me that this will all pass, that we are safe as long as we remain indoors.

I am so scared.

Signing off,

Artur Goldstein, aged ten

Rebecca sighed as she read the last paragraph, deep down inside something stirred in her. Could it be a conscience? She really didn't know. It was that same feeling she'd suppressed years ago, quarantined in her psyche in a place where it could never be used against her. She needed to be strong. After all it was just her against the world wasn't it? Wilf's first entry meant virtually nothing to her, they were just empty words written by a spoilt, frightened child with too much imagination.

She quickly pasted in the next entry:

10 November 1938, Berlin
Old Mr Zacchary from number 29 was taken away in the middle of the night by the SS. I overheard mama telling papa that it is no longer safe here. She told him she'd read something in the *Die Rote Fahne* newspaper about a Kinder Transport leaving for England sometime in November. She also mentioned some gold coins, but I couldn't quite hear her as Fritz was barking at people shouting in the street. I am still scared.
Signing off, Artur Goldstein, aged ten

Rebecca's heartbeat quickened and her eyes instantly lit up at the mention of *gold coins!* She decided to skip through the next eight entries to the last but one:

8 November 1938, Berlin Hauptbahnhof Train Station
I have just kissed mama and papa goodbye on the platform, the train has pulled away and I am crying. I wonder if I will ever see them again. The coat mama gave me is heavy, she

told me to keep it with me at all times, that the coat represented my freedom and not to open the lining until I'm safely in England.

I think I know what she has done, she has sewn the gold coins into the lining, I can feel them, I can even count them. There are twelve in total. I will keep my word if it's the last thing I do, and not open the lining until I reach England. I can't stop crying, there are hundreds of children here, they are all crying. The SS guards won't let anybody have any water or food, they keep laughing at us, calling us all the time filthy Jews. What is wrong with my country – does the Fuhrer know about this? I wonder.

I am so scared.

Signing off,

Artur Goldstein, aged ten

Finally, she was reading the last entry:

14 November 1938, Harwich, England

The crossing was terrible, the sea came right over the front of the ship in huge torrents, it was terrifying. The crew have been very kind to us and every few hours we are offered hot chocolate and sandwiches. Some of the children are seasick and Mr Shearer, the kindly old gentleman from below, spends most of his time mopping up the sick and telling us stories about how wonderful and free England is. A short time ago the captain announced we were now safely within the twelve-mile limit, and in sight of English shores.

I split open the lining and am now holding twelve shiny gold coins with the word "Liberty" written on their face surrounded by the stars and stripes and stamped on the back is the date, its 1838. They must be quite rare. I will hide them safely away in the lining of the suitcase mama kindly packed for me. I have to go now, the ship has just sounded three blasts of her horn, and I can see lights out of my porthole on the shore.

Not quite so scared now.

Signing off, Artur Goldstein, aged ten

Rebecca placed the phone down on her silky pink eiderdown engrossed in thought looking up at the ornately carved ceiling rose above her head.

So, where's this suitcase then Wilf? Where would you hide it?

She suddenly she remembered the note. The one Wilf placed under her door warning her to never enter his room unless invited. She mouthed it word by word as she lay there.

"Finally, Rebecca under no circumstances are you to ever enter my bedroom. You must always knock first, then wait for me to answer. You are never to enter without being invited."

Right then Wilf, it's curry night soon, you'll enjoy that. This one's on me, thought Rebecca…

7. Rebecca

Outside, the pavement was slippery and wet. Thankfully the overnight snow had stopped and was gradually being replaced by a grey muddy slush that sloshed up the sides of her black boots. Rebecca quickened her pace down Park Street.

Grey scattered clouds pushed along by high winds raced across the skyline above. The scene reminded her of the time when one of her so-called *uncles* had taken her to see "The Lion, the Witch and the Wardrobe" one rainy night in Bristol city centre. She loved the book, but thought the film was much better. Even as little girl sat there licking an ice cream in the front stalls, she didn't want to be Lucy Pevensie, or that twattish sister of hers, Susan. "No, not me!" She'd told one of her uncles. "I want to be the White Witch instead."

Approaching the busy intersection that separates Park Street and Park Row, she saw a reflection of a man holding a brolly in his hands in Boots' shop window opposite. It looked very much like the man she'd seen at the funeral. The same one who'd kept staring at her across the graveside.

"He's watching me, don't panic," she mumbled to herself quickening her pace. But the man just kept staring at her. She shouted across the street, "Hey, you over there! Yes, you! I can see you. I know you're…"

The man started to walk towards her and took a glance up and down the slush covered road as he folded his umbrella up on the crossing and shook it to the pavement as he approached. Rebecca stood frozen to the spot.

"Rebecca Susan Thorneycroft?" the man enquired.

"Yes, and who the hell are you? Are you stalking me? I'll scream, there's lots of people around," she anxiously replied.

The man didn't say a word, instead he reached into his pocket and pulled out a police-warrant card and dangled it two inches from her face.

"I am Detective Sergeant Andy McDermott of the Avon and Somerset Constabulary, Miss Thorneycroft."

Rebecca was trying hard to act normal, but her trembling hands betrayed her. She blew into her gloves and blamed the cold.

"Sorry, it's so bitterly cold today, isn't it? How can I help you Sergeant?" she asked, still blowing into her gloves.

"Well, I need to ask you a few questions. I was wondering if you wouldn't mind accompanying me to Redland police station."

"Questions, what sort of questions?" she snapped. *That was too quick Rebecca, too quick. Calm yourself down girl.*

"Well, I think that might be better answered under caution down at the police station, don't you?" he replied, pausing for a moment before offering her a choice. A sort of lifeline. "But if that's not convenient we could always grab a coffee and have an informal chat off the record. What do you say?"

He fancies me. He's trying not to show it, but he can't make up his mind whether he prefers my fanny or my tits.

"Well I must admit I could do with something warm inside me, especially in this weather. So, coffee it is then Sergeant, lead the way." *He liked that one. He's a bit overweight, a tad old for my liking, but not that bad looking. We'll see Rebecca, just keep playing the game. We'll see.*

"Okay, good, that's probably your best option, the sooner we get this wrapped up the sooner I can close the file. I've parked my car behind the coffee shop down on the next corner, so the coffees on me, come on."

Rebecca didn't respond, but instead pouted, licking her top lip invitingly, she smiled at him. *He seemed to like that.*

They both walked the next twenty yards to the café in total silence as Rebecca thought, *better a numbing silence than mindless babbling. Mustn't let him see how scared I am.*

Opening the café door, McDermott stood to one side allowing her to brush passed. "Latte Rebecca? he asked. "You don't mind me calling you Rebecca, do you? You can call me Andy if you like."

"Thank you, Andy," she replied as he closed the door behind her.

Rebecca took a seat by the window facing the road. The wind was howling up and down the street as snow drifted across the roof tops fluttering its way to the pavement below.

A few people who'd managed to venture out reminded her of something Lowry may once have painted with their collars pulled taught beneath their knees, bent forward struggling to walk up the ice-covered hill.

Holding two steaming cups of coffee, McDermott sat down and shuffled along the bench seat towards hers.

"Okay, fire away Andy," she said. "How can I help you?" she asked purposely, admiring the scene and pretending she didn't give a hoot what he wanted.

"Well this is strictly off the record at the moment Rebecca, so I'm not taking any notes or recording you. Just try and relax and answer the questions as honestly and truthfully as you can, okay?"

That was rehearsed.

"Okay, that's fine Andy, go ahead," she said, still staring out through the frosted-up window.

"Now, a couple of weeks ago we had an Elizabeth, uh…" McDermott said forgetting her surname, flicking through his untidy notebook.

"Baker," Rebecca answered, a little too quickly for her own liking.

"Yes, Baker. You obviously know this Mrs Baker then?"

"Yes, of course I do, I used to work for her mother, Aunt Mae. Sorry, I meant Mrs Mae Wilson."

"Okay, Mrs Baker seems to think there was something very odd about her mother's death, and she doesn't understand why her mother left you a hundred and seventy-five grand, considering you'd only worked for her for what…" he said, flicking the page over on his untidy notebook.

"Just over two years," Rebecca answered calmly, sipping her hot coffee. *Believe me, it felt soooo much longer.*

McDermott's detective senses were already on high alert and he sat deep in thought for a moment. *She's playing this too cool. She's definitely hiding something; I can feel it. Okay, we'll try something else.*

"Well two years is a long time I suppose. So, in all that time did Mrs Baker ever mention anything about including you in her will? I mean, you must admit that's an awful lot of money to leave to a… sorry no offence meant… but a carer."

Rebecca thought she knew where he was going with this line of questioning, but she'd had enough and decided it was time to challenge him. *When you're on the ropes, go on the offensive*, she thought. So, she did.

"No offence taken at all Sergeant. But unless you've got something substantial, something you think connects me with Mrs Wilson's untimely death then I suggest you either charge me or let me go. Thanks for the coffee Sergeant. I really enjoyed our little chat, but I must be off."

Rebecca got up and was about to pick up her handbag when McDermott placed his hand on her arm and pushed her back down onto the seat.

"Sit down Rebecca, just one last question then you can go. When was the last time you saw or spoke to your stepfather, Tom Thorneycroft?"

Rebecca knew she couldn't admit to seeing him. If he was brought in for questioning, he'd sing like a canary and blame her for everything. So, a blunt denial seemed to be her only option.

"I haven't seen or spoken to my stepfather for at least three years Sergeant. We are what you might term "estranged" at the moment. So, if that will be all, I'd like…"

McDermott smiled and removed a photograph of her and Tom Thorneycroft having coffee at the Bridge Café just a few weeks before. The photograph was as clear as a bell, he could even make out the contents of Tom's pasty the clarity was that good. So, Rebecca sat back down again and huffed as McDermott shuffled himself even closer along the bench towards her.

"So, you're lying and that on its own is enough to pull you in for further questioning Rebecca. How do you feel about that? I mean, you know old Tom Thorneycroft, never could keep his mouth shut, could he? Probably drop you in it the minute we pull him in. So, I'll give you a choice Rebecca, you see I don't want to have to deal with all the paperwork that's involved in exhuming a body. That wouldn't be good news for anyone now, would it?"

He's threating me. Exhuming a body!

"Exhuming, what do you mean exhuming, I did…"

"It's easy for us to find out what really happened Rebecca, but I have a hunch you already know that, and you know what really happened to Mrs Wilson, don't you! I'm right, aren't I?"

He knows, shit. The overdose, it would still show up. I knew she should have been cremated.

"Exhume away Sergeant," Rebecca replied as confidently as she was able. "Aunt Mae died of a heart attack! It's as simple as that. She was eighty bloody seven."

"Okay, let's try, again shall we?" he said, clicking his thumb and forefinger together an inch from her face, moving himself to within touching distance. Then, lowering his voice to just above a whisper, he placed his hand on the top of her thigh and gently rubbed it.

"Now, Rebecca I can make all of this go away, just like that," he said, clicking his fingers again. "That is for twenty-five grand and a good shag now and then. So, what do you say? Hey."

His breath stunk of cigarettes and alcohol. His eyes were wanton as he adjusted himself on the bench seat, turned and joined her staring out of the window. He was smiling, clearly satisfied with himself.

He's won, he's got me right where he wants me and he knows it, there no way out. Just sit and think for a minute, stall him for a few seconds. But it was hopeless, and she knew it. By then a sense of reality had set. He only had to pull Tom in, exhume the body and she'd be looking at a life sentence.

If they dig her up, I'm finished? So, what choice do I have?

Then, turning towards him and looking him straight in the eye, she told him exactly what he wanted to hear.

"Sounds like we've got a deal then Andy," she replied as calmly as she could, all the while faking a smile, flashing her long eye lashes and drawing his hand very slowly up the inside of her skirt.

"Right that's better," he said, almost purring. "Now we've got that bit out of the way we can get down to business. Now my guess is that this isn't the first time you've done this now is it? I've been studying your file for a while now and I want in on the next one, I want a cut of the profits. I also want our little arrangement to go on and on. You see Rebecca this is just the start."

"You know this is bloody blackmail, don't you?" she answered, trying to resurrect a small semblance of self-respect.

"Yeah, and that carries what?" McDermott said looking up at the ceiling tiles above. "Eight nine years max? But murder, now that's a totally different ball game altogether. That carries a life sentence. So, think about it for a minute, a quick shag now and then and a cut of the kitty. Surely you must realise that's a small price to pay to keep you and your old man out of the nick. This way everyone's a winner."

"You're a bastard McDermott!" Rebecca snarled, purposely using his surname for the first time.

"I know, my old man used to say that," was his brief retort literally laughing in her face.

"So, back to my flat then is it?" he asked, rolling his tongue like a jackal on heat.

Rebecca was desperately trying to find a way out. She needed time to think. "I can't today," she replied. "I have to be back by four. So, not enough time I'm afraid."

"There's always time Rebecca, my cars parked out the back so why don't you get that murdering ass of yours into it right now! Before I lose my fucking temper!"

Fuck! Shit. Play along, Rebecca, just do as he says.

"Okay, calm down, at least let me finish my latte. You really are an impatient bastard McDermott."

As far as he was concerned play time was over. He gripped her by the arm yanking her towards him. "Follow me," he said through gritted teeth as he literally marched her out of the café.

Parked just around the back in the corner of the snow-covered car park was his beat-up old Audi A4 convertible, with a sagging black roof.

"Looks like this has seen better days," said Rebecca light heartedly as she walked towards it, hoping that he'd see some sense and change his mind. But he didn't, instead he unlocked the driver's door and they both got in.

The rough leather seat felt cold against the top of her thighs as they both sat in silence for a minute looking out through the frost-covered windscreen. McDermott started the engine. The inside of the car was freezing, as was Rebecca.

"Right, Rebecca," he said looking across at her and rubbing his hands together. "Now you and I are going to have some fun, so why don't you take off that tight little skirt of yours and let me have a look at the goods."

"Don't you treat me like some bloody whore you bastard!" she shouted while she unzipped the side of her skirt, pulling it down into the foot-well. "We might have an arrangement as you like to call it! But don't you push me too far. Or I might just take the chance of a fucking exhumation."

"Okay, okay, calm down will you!" he replied, placing his hand between her cold thighs pulling at the sides of her black French knickers. In micro-seconds his fingers were inside her feeling and probing the inside of her vagina as he struggled to pull his trousers down with his other hand, eventually revealing a pair of saggy old pair of white Y-fronts with red piping on the fly. She could see he was aroused.

Just think of anything, just get it over and done with you bastard! Tomorrow's another day, she thought as tears welled up in her eyes.

"Touch my cock, touch it!" he demanded through gritted teeth.

So, she did. Then his head went down between her legs and she thought he was going to lick her. But instead he reached down, pushed the seat further back then climbed onto her while yanking at her knickers and pulling them down into the footwell. Rebecca thought she heard them rip.

With one violent bodily thrust he entered her. She could feel his heavy weight on her body as he pushed and pushed forcing his hard penis deeper and deeper into her dryness. His acrid breath washed over her face as he greedily suckled her neck and fought for her breasts in a frenzy. He was thrusting himself into her at the same time as holding one of her legs up against the frozen windscreen.

A workman strolled passed holding a shovel to clear the snow. He didn't look in. She looked at him as he worked. She wanted to scream, but she couldn't. *Stay calm, let him finish, you've been here before Rebecca remember. Just let the bastard finish.*

All of a sudden, his jerking intensified and, as his head bent backwards and away, his nostrils flared as he let out a moan and she felt his wet warmth enter her body and knew it was almost over. He tried to kiss her lips as he was coming, but she turned her face away. He instead sucked her neck and fondled her breasts. He let out a last lingering moan and finally he was finished. She could feel his heaving chest on top of her rapidly breathing in and out.

He was smiling but he didn't say a word. Instead he just nodded his head as he pulled himself off. She pushed his heavy body back onto his own seat as she started to pull her knickers up. They were ripped at the sides and his wet semen was dribbling down the inside of her thighs. But the animal still sat in his seat smiling as he did his trousers up. He thought it was funny, after all he was in control. And McDermott relished control.

"So that's that then, got what you wanted in the end didn't you?" she snapped twisting and turning her body in the cramped confines of the leather seat as she attempted to zip up her skirt.

He suddenly looked across and, without any warning, reached over and clutched her by the chin and held it between his large hands as his warm stale breath washed over her. The cruelty in his eyes issued a warning.

"Better than the nick though ain't it, eh Rebecca?" he spouted. "And don't forget you work for me now. Make sure you tell your old man that. I'm in and I want twenty-five grand in cash. Got it? So, why don't you just fuck off and I'll be in touch in a few days. I've got your number from records so keep your mobile on. And don't forget, one little word from me and you're both nicked."

He released her chin, reached across, unlocked the car door and pushed her out onto the icy pavement throwing her handbag after her. Rebecca was shaking from head to foot.

Mustn't see me crying, she thought as she walked off feeling more like a dirty whore who'd just earned twenty-five quid, rather than given away twenty-five grand. She could feel his eyes watching her from behind as she straightened her coat. The biting wind was freezing as her tears ran freely down her cheeks. Her hands were as cold as her heart as she walked across the ice-covered car park. His car raced passed throwing up a black watery slush as it screeched around the corner and headed back down Park Street.

McDermott didn't look back and a seething Rebecca vowed to herself, *I'll get you for this you fucker! You just wait and see if I don't. Give me some time then we'll see just how clever you are. You prick!*

She looked at her watch and realised she was going to be late meeting Tom. So, running as quickly as she could trying not to slip over and, with grey mush whipping the back of her black boots, she sprinted towards the café door at the bottom of the snow-covered street. As she arrived, she could see the unmistakeable shape of Tom's outline through the curved Georgian window as he sat there waiting, fiddling with his jacket. Like he always did if she was late.

Hearing the café door open, Tom immediately looked around and for a moment the briefest of smiles crossed his haggard looking face. But less than a second later the same look was replaced with a frown. He gestured with his hand signalling for her to sit down.

"Sit down, sit, what's up?" he said. "You look like shit. Tell me what's happened?"

"Something terrible has happened! Something really bloody awful," she replied, trying to hold back tears as she placed her wet handbag on the spare seat. Tom was constantly scanning the room as she tried to catch her breath. Then, satisfied nobody was really taking any notice, he returned his attention to her and asked again.

"Tell me! What the fuck happened?" he demanded.

"I've just been raped," she cried out through gnarled lips panting like a wet dog, holding her chest and trying to steady her breathing. She sat still for a few moments with her head bowed playing nervously with the hem of her coat. Sniffing as grief was replaced with an uncontrollable rage causing her to grind her shiny white teeth as she looked at him through watery eyes and began to explain.

"Do you remember that man I told you about," she said blowing her nose. "You know the one I saw at Aunt Mae's funeral? The one that was staring at me?"

"What man? Who? When…?" Tom asked, screwing his face up, clearly unsure what the hell she was talking about.

"I thought I told you, maybe I didn't or maybe you just weren't listening as usual. Anyway, there was a man at the funeral standing behind that bitch Eliz-A-Beth and her husband Mikey. He just stood the entire time staring, looking me up and down. It was really creepy."

"Then the second I looked over to see what he was looking at he'd smile and pull his umbrella back down over his face. Weird don't you think? I thought he was one of the family who'd taken a fancy to me. Well guess what? I've just met him again, right here today on the corner of Park Row, and he's only a fucking copper!"

"How do you know that?" Tom spat back in panic.

"Because he shoved his fucking warrant card in my face, then went on to tell me that he knows all about Aunt Mae, and how he's going to have her dug up unless we hand over twenty-five grand in cash. Shit! Shit! He knows all about us. He knows! What are we gonna do?"

Rebecca broke down crying again holding her hands to her face. But as always, and totally in character, Tom was less than sympathetic.

"Keep your bloody voice down will you!" he shouted. "Shush, calm yourself down you stupid cow! Stop and think for a minute girl," was Tom's sympathetic offering as he ran his tobacco-stained fingers through his grey greasy hair and banged his large fist down on the table in anger.

"Fuck off, none of your business!" he yelled at the other patrons, who all looked away, a few prematurely asking for their bill.

"Then he raped me!" she mumbled, this time in a much quieter tone. "It happened in his car about twenty minutes ago, he's a right bastard! He knows all about us. What if he finds out about the rest? They'd never let us out. They'd throw away the key. Oh God what are we going to do?"

"What's his name Rebecca? Tell me his bloody name."

"His name is Andy McDermott and he's a Detective Sergeant in the CID, from Redland nick."

"Never heard of him., Tom angrily replied as he stroked his stubbled chin. "What else did he say to you?"

"He said our arrangement, as he put it, was going to be *on-going* and he wants in on all our future…" Rebecca swallowed hard searching her mind for the right description of their unusual trade. But couldn't.

"Yes, go on, future what?" Tom stupidly demanded.

"Murders," she answered, breaking down again. "You know fucking murder! That's what we do, isn't it?"

But Tom didn't bat an eyelid, not even at the mention of the word. Instead he was deep in thought as he sat planning his next move.

"Okay, I've an idea and, if we pull it off, we'll have him by the bollocks. Where and when does he want to collect the money… this twenty-five grand?"

"Well, he said he'd call me first and tell me where and what time to meet him."

"Right, the second he calls you; you call me okay. I'll video him taking the money. I've still got that Nikon long-range video camera I nicked out of Mae's house after I poisoned her. So, don't worry, we'll get the bastard. Andy bloody McDermott just picked on the wrong family. The Thorneycroft's don't roll over for anyone," Tom said, wringing his hands like a seasoned street fighter before a big fight.

He doesn't give a shit about the rape, or me come to that, does he? But he'll make damn sure a bent copper like Andy bloody McDermott doesn't deprive him of his precious twenty-five grand. He reminds me of a modern day "Fagin." In fact, that was what the judge called him when he was up for benefits fraud – "A modern-day Fagin."

In a way, I suppose over the years I've sort of become his "Oliver," but not for too much longer you bastard! Oh no, this needs to end somewhere. But that bastard McDermott needs sorting first…

8. McDermott

McDermott's early morning meeting with his immediate superior DS Peter Goodfield, or "guv" as Peter preferred to be called, was scheduled for eight o'clock sharp. Peter Goodfield was a career copper and, aged thirty-eight, was seven years younger than McDermott and, with a University degree under his belt, had overtaken him on the promotional front years ago.

Peter really enjoyed their master–servant relationship. He liked nothing more than to relax at home in his brown leather armchair with his hands neatly folded across his toned stomach, spouting off to his wife Julie about how amusing it was to lord over such lesser mortals like Andy McDermott.

Peter despised Andy McDermott and everything he stood for.

"*Knock, knock.*"

"Come in Andy, the door is open."

"Morning guv," McDermott said as he walked in and placed his steaming hot coffee mug straight down on the top of Peter's tidy desk. Peter immediately picked it up and quickly slid a piece of A4 paper underneath, shaking his hand, feigning a burn. McDermott utterly despised Peter bloody *perfect* Goodfield.

We're off to a good start then, thought McDermott.

"Right Andy, apart from being eight minutes late and nearly burning my bloody hand off, what have you got for me? How did you get on with that Thorneycroft woman? I took another look at her file this morning. Tasty looking bird, isn't she? The old man's a right ugly bastard though, hey?"

McDermott laughed at his guvnor's remark. He enjoyed the game and after all he was the one who'd be twenty-five grand up in a minute.

"Yeah, must admit nice bit of tottee that one, but you're right the old man's a right nasty piece of work. Seasoned old jailbird that one. Got a list of offences as long as my arm," McDermott said tapping his nose for effect as Peter nodded and sat back in his chair, his hands neatly folded across his stomach.

Peter really enjoyed being told he was right, but felt the game was so much better when he'd manipulated McDermott into conceding he was right.

"Well," McDermott said, "We had a nice little chat over a coffee yesterday morning and she told me she really loved the old dear and she hasn't seen hide nor hair of Tom Thorneycroft in months. According to her, this daughter Elizabeth… whatever her name is… had it in for her from day one. So, if you want my opinion guv, I think we're barking up the wrong tree. I think this Elizabeth… what's her surname again?"

"Baker! For God's sake McDermott, it's bloody Baker!" Peter snapped, clearly annoyed that McDermott had not only forgotten her surname twice, but he hadn't even bothered to bring the case file in.

"Yeah, Baker, sorry that's it, well like you said guv I think it's all sour grapes. You were right all along. You know the jealousy thing and all that." Before continuing, McDermott decided to choose his next words very carefully.

"So, it all seems a bit *Johnny upright* to me, I reckon she's pissed off that she's lost a hundred and seventy-five grand. And that's that."

McDermott stared across the desk waiting for a reaction, but Peter just sat reading, holding the cover of the file between his thumb and forefinger.

Just sit and wait… Let the prick reach his own conclusions. Let him think he was right all along, McDermott thought waiting for Peter's response.

"Okay, wrap it all up then and close the file. Like I said before, it all sounds like sour grapes to me. Make sure you file it away with Veronica in records. I mean you never know, even I can be wrong sometimes."

Peter was the one to feign a laugh this time.

"Doubt that very much guv," McDermott replied patronisingly, the ass licking statement causing Peter to glare across the desk at him suspiciously.

Shit! Bridge too far that one! Never mind, time to bugger off.

"Well if that'll be all guv, there's a stack of stuff on my desk I need to look at," was McDermott's final remark as he rose from the chair. But McDermott's last comment had lit Peter's touch paper.

"Yes, I know Andy, I put them all there, remember! So, start getting some results will you. Results Andy! That'll be all for now. Oh, and next time you come in make sure you have a shave first. If DCI Cook sees you looking like that there'll be hell to play."

"Will do guv," McDermott replied faking a two-fingered salute, stroking his stubbled chin before closing the door quietly behind him.

In the outer office, Veronica was standing on the top rung of her steps filing away long forgotten case files as McDermott emerged from Peter's office. His first thoughts as he studied her form were, *she isn't half bad that one, not for a fifty-year-old bird. Must explore that possibility another time.*

"This one's dead Veronica, guvnor said to shred it," McDermott said showing her the case file in his hand.

"Just leave it over there will you Andy, put it on top of that pile on my desk. They're all going to be shredded later."

"Thanks Veronica, cracking pair of legs by the way girl."

"Bugger off McDermott, you say that to all the girls."

McDermott shrugged off the comment offering nothing more than a cheeky wink as he walked to the back of the station and pushed the heavy blue doors open, before pacing the five yards to the smoking shelter at the bottom of the frost-covered lawn.

Outside he could hear a prisoner shouting and swearing from the cells as one of the uniformed officers delivered his breakfast of a mug of warm tea and a single slice of burnt toast. He chuckled to himself, happy that his days spent attending to drunken, drugged up wasters was a long way behind him.

Lighting one of his favourite Gitane's, his mouth savoured the warmth of the strong French tobacco, drawing the smoke deep into his lungs as he looked down at his watch. He glanced over to check the blue doors were still closed and took a quick gulp from his hip flask. The same one his father had engraved for him with the words *Top Bobby* after passing out of police college years ago. But that was back then, when they were still on talking terms. McDermott missed his father.

Looking up towards the hoary greyness, watching the clouds rush across the sky, he stamped his feet, shuddering in the coldness of the morning wondering if more snow might be on its way.

Either way, he'd have a shave first. And then he'd call Rebecca. She'd like that…

9. Tom

It would have been highly unusual and completely out of character for an old jailbird like Tom Thorneycroft to wake up without a hangover and this particular morning was no different to any other. As he sat up, he rubbed his eyes and looked across from the warmth of his grubby bed at his bedside cabinet.

The alarm clock told him it was 9.45 am. And as usual Tom Thorneycroft felt, smelt, and looked like shit. He sat up, reached over and picked up an unfinished can of warm Pilsner lager and gulping down a warm mouthful he lit his first cigarette of the day. Using the upturned cap of a spent deodorant spray as an ashtray he laid back and balanced it precariously on his chest. He lay quite motionless for a moment watching as the silver-grey smoke formed circles above his head.

"All right! So, bloody what! I've got nearly ninety grand stashed away. But what good is it to me! I can't buy a house or a new car with it, can I? I can't even put it in the bank or rent a decent flat. Not without that nosey bastard probation officer!

That interfering do-gooding twat Colin fuckin' Andrews getting onto me."

Tom could almost hear him.

"Come on Tom, tell me where all this money came from? Come on. Better you tell me now?"

"Fuck off Colin!" Tom yelled at the top of his voice releasing a retching cough from his filth-ridden bed, as his second-hand iPhone rang on the bedside table. Stubbing out his half-smoked cigarette in the deodorant lid and supporting his weight with his elbow, he leant across the bed, picked up the phone and placed it to his ear.

"Hello Becks, has he rung?" he asked.

"Yep, he's rung."

"Good, when?"

"A few minutes ago. He wants to meet me on the corner of Princess Street in about an hour, just behind the Theatre Royal in Bath."

"Okay, that'll be what?" Tom asked, checking his watch. "Smack on eleven o'clock," he replied releasing a loud wailing yawn as he placed his feet down on the grotty sick-stained carpet.

"I'll be there. You won't see me; I'll keep out of sight. Just make sure you hand over the money in the sleeves the bank gave it to you in. Whatever happens don't put it in a bag. I want a nice clear video of him handling the cash."

"All right… Do you reckon this'll work? I'm shitting myself."

"Just you leave it to me Becks, I've handled bigger fish than this wanker. Don't worry this will be over soon, you mark my words."

"Call me as soon as it's done, will you?" she asked.

"Will do, you'll be the first to know, bye, see you later, okay."

"Yeah, okay, bye."

Placing the phone down on his filthy blue eiderdown, he rose from his bed and as usual couldn't be bothered to wash or even brush his teeth. So, sniffing his armpits he decided a wash could wait until his return.

Stuffing the long-range Nikon camera into its leather case, he caught a glimpse of himself in the cracked wall mirror. Pointing at his reflection, he talked to it.

"Here I come McDermott you bastard!" he yelled at the top of his voice. "Nobody rips Tom Thorneycroft off. Nobody!"

Forty minutes later, as he crouched down behind two stinking wheelie bins he removed the camera from its leather case. Checking the green light was on, lifting it into position and balancing its weight on his shoulder he placed the lens firmly against his eye. Then pressing the auto-focus button, the motor *whirled* and *whined* as it extended its length and he had a clear, unobstructed view of the corner of Princess Street from the rear of Saw Close.

He could see Rebecca standing on the opposite corner wearing her long black coat with its fake mole-skin collar. Her shiny black hair was swinging from left to right as she stood gripping hold of her black Mulberry handbag like her life depended on it. Strangers passed by wrapped up in thick winter clothing as Tom admired her sleek and shapely curves allowing his thoughts to drift for a moment. *"Lovely, ah Tom, I'd pay for that I would,"* he whispered rolling his tongue, his cold breath scattering in the morning air. *Concentrate! He'll be here in a minute.* He'd swear he could almost smell him. Then suddenly without warning everything around him darkened as a shadow was cast from behind, altering the light that entered the lens, so he gently lowered the camera to his knee and looked up searching the grey sky for the offending cloud, or the large bird that might be passing over. And then he saw him.

"Hello Tommy boy! Well, well, you dirty old scumbag! Thought I might find you here," McDermott said grabbing him by the collar, pulling him backwards as he dragged him out on to the busy street. Tom looked up and pulled the camera tighter to his chest.

"Get the fuck off me, you bastard," he shouted only to be rewarded by a hard kick in the chest by McDermott. "I'll take that Tommy boy, c'mon hand it over," he demanded, back-handing him across the face. "You're a wanker Thorneycroft! You and that slut of a stepdaughter of yours are now up shit creek without a paddle."

Pulling him to his feet, still gripping him by the collar, McDermott heard the lining split on Tom's jacket and stood there smugly eyeing him up and down watching as the colour drained from his face, faster than piss from a flushed toilet.

Then without saying another word he coiled the leather camera strap around his hand and started to laugh.

Rebecca was waiting to cross the street, watching the most terrifying man she'd ever encountered cowering like a scolded dog with McDermott stood over him, gripping his collar.

"How'd you know I was here?" Tom said looking up and glaring at McDermott.

"Because I'm the old bill you wanker and you walked right into it. You've done exactly what I thought you'd do. That's why I chose this spot in the first place. Plank! You're really getting too old for this. You should know better at your age."

Tom shook his head in blank resignation and for the first time wondered if McDermott was right. *Was he getting too old?*

Rebecca was standing just a few feet behind with her arms folded, and decided to ask him outright:

"So, what happens now? I mean you're a lot of things McDermott, but you aren't stupid. You're not going to take us down to the station and hand over all this lovely money, now are you? So, tell me what are you going to do?" she asked confidently, swinging her Mulberry bag left then right.

"She's the one with the brains Tommy," McDermott stated. "Clever bird this step-daughter of yours," he said as he released Tom's collar and pushed him back down in-between the filthy bins in disgust.

"Tell you what, Rebecca, let's go off and have a nice little chat eh?" he said, rolling his tongue. "I think it's about time we renegotiated our terms, don't you? What do you think Tom?" he asked.

But Tom decided he was safer on the pavement and just sat there like a scolded dog, without replying…

10. Gold

Rebecca was knelt down in the grand lounge polishing one of Wilf's matching brass candlesticks that adorned his elegant marble fireplace. Her thoughts were elsewhere as she shined, polishing the shaft to a brightness even a stickler like Wilf Kennedy would admire. She could feel herself getting angrier and angrier as she continually wiped and wiped, and a seething hatred like a physical disease infected every inch of her body. She fought the urge to smash the candlestick into the fireplace. She wanted to kill McDermott, savage him for what he'd done to her. But she could wait. Her time would come. The man was living on borrowed time.

I can wait as long as it takes. But you're going to pay. Oh, you are going to pay. Her mind was in a turmoil, each twisted thought was centred on how she was going to kill him, how he'd suffer the way she was suffering. Her whole body shuddered as she imagined him writhing around on top of her thrusting himself deeper and deeper, his acrid breath washing over her.

She placed the gleaming candlestick down onto the hearth as her thoughts returned to the coins. *Where is he hiding them?*

Where would I hide them? To Rebecca, finding the coins would enable her to escape this dreadful life she was forced to lead.

I could smash the bedroom door in! she thought. *Grab the coins and be done with it. But what if they're not in there? What happens then? Smashed in door. On the run. No job. Nowhere to go… Fuck!*

Rebecca stood up, untied her apron string, opened the lounge door and heard Wilf on the landing above whistling the same monotonous tune he always whistled if he was excited about something. *Another lunch maybe? Another banquet with Lord and Lady bloody kiss my ass*, she thought as Wilf shouted down the stairs.

"Rebecca! Is that you I can hear down there? I seem to have mislaid my silk tie. You know the one, the one I always wear when I'm having brunch with Lord and Lady Asquith. The gold one. Have you seen it anywhere?"

"Yes Wilf…" she replied, fed up to the back teeth with his constant demands. "It's pressed and hanging on the parlour door. Shall I fetch it for you?" she asked, letting out a gentle sigh.

"No, that's very gracious of you Rebecca. I'll be down in a minute, so I can grab it then. Thanks anyway," he replied as he toddled off.

So, going out again are we then Wilf? Think I'll take a look in that room of yours.

Less than half an hour later Rebecca was waving from the open doorway as Wilf's Rolls Royce glided through the gates and disappeared. Finally, she was *home alone*. Quickly closing the front door and taking five giant leaps like a bat out of hell she ran up the stairs, sprinted along the landing and coming to a halt outside Wilf's bedroom door. She rattled the handle, but the door was made of solid oak and had two Yale locks fitted top and bottom. The door hardly moved.

He must have a spare set of keys somewhere, she thought, biting away at her bottom lip.

Parlour? No that's too obvious. Scullery, that too. Kitchen? Office? No! So where, Rebecca, think! What rooms aren't used? Actually, why is it he won't let me light a fire in the downstairs dining room. Why? And at that moment it came to her... she knew.

Racing back down the stairs faster than she'd run up, she sprinted along the highly polished parquet floor and reached the dining room – the same room in which she is forbidden to light a fire.

For the briefest of moments, she looked both behind her and at the front door. The house was deathly quiet, apart from the distant rumble of light traffic outside. So, turning the handle and entering the room she knelt down on all fours in front of the hearth, then poked her head up the dark chimney.

At first, she couldn't see a thing, just a sooty black hole that seemed to disappear around a bend somewhere into nothingness. Gently wiping her fingers around the inside of the brickwork she was rewarded by a scattering of thick black soot and hollow twigs falling harmlessly onto her head, before bouncing onto the hearth below. Coughing and spluttering, she waited for the dust to settle, then once more looked inside.

It was pitch black. She could just about make out a bend where the old Victorian brickwork changed direction. She suddenly let out a scream as an old bird's nest with three chick carcasses hanging out from either side fluttered harmlessly into the hearth below. Visibly shaken, she brushed the carcasses aside and returned her attention to the chimney. She saw it!

She saw something that wasn't supposed to be there. A small box! A metal box was balancing precariously on top of the brickwork shelf just two feet above her head and within touching distance, within reach.

She reached up, grabbed its thin metal handle, trembling as she removed it from the chimney. She could hear something metallic rattling around inside as she placed the box on her knee, blew off the soot and opened the lid. Her face instantly lit up as she noticed two shiny brass keys inside.

Discarding the box, she left the room with keys in hand and went to wash herself in the downstairs bathroom. She realised she was covered in soot and grime.

Scrubbing the sink out afterwards and pulling on a set of Marigold gloves, she took off again up the stairs and once more ran along the landing like a woman possessed. She tried inserting the first key into the door's top lock, but it didn't fit. She swapped keys and immediately the top lock gave way. Using her weight to push against the door, she turned the second key in the bottom lock, and it worked. The heavy oak door swung open.

She recoiled as that all too familiar smell of Wilf's favourite Old Spice after shave invaded her nasal senses. The whole room reeked of it. The curtains were drawn tightly, so the room was in complete darkness. Reaching over, she flicked on the light switch and saw that the entire length of his dressing room table was covered in at least a dozen black and white pictures, set within their own ornate gold frames, containing what she assumed were deceased family members. At the other end of the room she noticed a portable computer screen with a thin wire attached. The wire had been neatly pushed through a tiny hole in the side of the wardrobe and as she opened the door she could see that the wire had been clipped to the back of the wooden panel, then pushed through a hole in the party wall that separated her room from Wilf's.

I fuckin' knew it! You are a disgusting old Bastard! She felt compelled to rip out the wire, but she stopped herself and began to think.

If I rip it out, he'll know I've been here. Tonight's curry night, she thought. *So, you enjoy those last few memories of me dancing naked around in my bedroom Wilf, because I'm going to kill you. You disgust me!*

Laying at the bottom of the wardrobe was a small leather suitcase that had obviously seen better days. It had a thick leather strap wrapped tightly around. She picked it up and, just as she had with the metal box, she shook it. It sounded empty, so she placed it down on the end of the bed, quickly unbuckled the leather strap and then, as she pushed both of the rusty old metal locks across, it emitted a loud *clunking* sound as the top sprang open.

Gingerly and very slowly she lifted the lid. Inside there was nothing. It was empty, apart from some old stained newspaper cuttings that looked like they dated back to the war years. She ran her fingers across the soft silky lining beneath the lid and felt something solid concealed in the top right-hand corner. She very carefully tried to ease back the purple lining, but the ancient material simply disintegrated in her hands. An old envelope had been secured to the right-hand corner, with the words *Reich Bank* written in bold type across the front. Below, there was the unmistakeable symbol of a golden Nazi swastika.

Using her long nails as talons, she scratched away at the envelope and felt huge satisfaction as the envelope fell apart and twelve shiny gold coins fell out rattling and rolling as they dropped down inside the old suitcase.

"Bingo! Yes! Yes!" she bellowed at the top of her voice, instantly regretting her sudden outburst and turning her attention to the gleaming coins laying so invitingly in front of her. Gathering them up she counted them into her apron pocket and less than fifteen minutes later she had managed to tuck the lining back into place. She buckled up the old suitcase and replaced it in exactly the same position she'd found it. Then she closed the wardrobe door, carefully pulling the camera wire as taught as she'd found it. Then stopping for a moment, checking for any tell-tale signs of entry, she pulled the bedroom door shut and ran back downstairs, tugging at the Marigold gloves off as she went.

At around four o'clock that afternoon, Rebecca was smiling sweetly as Wilf staggered in through the door three sheets to the wind, slurring through his arrival.

"I fink I'll have a little lie down Becca," he told her. "I've had a wonderful time. But a few to many bloody sherberts I'm afraid old girl. I'll leave you to organise dinner, shall I?"

Wilf's question was rhetorical of course so responded with nothing more than a wry smile. She took him by the arm and walked him up the stairs to bed.

"It's curry night tonight Wilf," Rebecca cheerfully announced as she walked him down the landing, her arm under this shoulder supporting his weight. "Shall I pop down to Abdul's later and pick one up?" she asked.

"Yes, yes, you do that Becca. You'll find some money in the kitchen cabinet. Give me a knock awound seven will you. Must say, you do look rather bloody stunning today Becca," Wilf's slurred as he stumbled through his bedroom door and passed out on the bed.

At seven o'clock sharp, Rebecca gave the customary three hard knocks and listened at the door. She could hear him yawning and stumbling around so, satisfied he was up, she returned to the dining room to set the table.

At around seven thirty Wilf, looking rather spent and wearing a set of striped pyjamas underneath his long blue housecoat, sat down at the formal dining table, taking a lunging gulp of his favourite cabernet before boldly declaring:

"Ah that's better Rebecca! he said, licking his lips. "Nothing like hair of the dog is there?"

Rebecca didn't answer. She was busily spooning Wilf's nut-free cauliflower curry onto a plate in the kitchen, the one she'd picked up earlier from Abdul at the Aziz.

"There you go Wilf," she said, placing the steaming hot vegetable curry down in front of him. "Once you've eaten that you'll feel much better. I'll go and finish the dishes, just shout when you've finished. I've got you a nice chocolate ice cream for dessert."

"You really are a little gem Rebecca. I don't know what I'd do without you. Must say this curry smells rather good," Wilf admitted as he inhaled a great lung full.

As she walked to the kitchen to start the washing up, Rebecca thought, *if it hadn't been for that hidden bloody camera, I might have felt sorry for you.* But she didn't because, like all the men she'd ever met, Wilf had lied and was trying to have her believe he was a kindly old man. So, like the rest, he had to go and that was that. Rebecca Thorneycroft needed to get on with her life. *So just choke you bastard. After all, you've had your life haven't you.*

As she was scrubbing the worktops down, using a neat bleach to clear away any evidence of the ground almonds she'd mixed into Wilf's curry, she thought she heard a shout followed by a loud crashing noise from the dining room. She chose to ignore it and instead turned the volume up on her Alexa. *There's nothing better than listening to a good old-fashioned cookery programme when you're happy, now is there?*

Up bright and breezy the following morning, Rebecca initially called an ambulance. This was followed by quite a scene as she screamed and cried on the phone to the police, informing them that she'd woken to find Wilf's dead body lying on the dining room floor.

Following normal protocol, about eight or nine minutes later two uniformed police officers, accompanied by two paramedics, arrived at the house. An hour later, whimpering beneath the relative safety of a heavy woollen blanket, Rebecca was completing her statement, telling the WPC how delightful Wilf had been and how he'd been a sort of mentor to her.

The following day, sadly Abdul and his head chef were arrested on suspicion of manslaughter and his business shut down, pending further investigation…

11. Enid

"Have you brought your references with you Rebecca?"

"I have Mrs Williams, they're right here," Rebecca calmly replied as Enid took the folded piece of paper from her hand and placed it face up on the glass coffee table.

"What a beautiful house Mrs Williams, it's so elegant," said a beaming Rebecca, glancing around the room admiring the high Edwardian ceilings and delicately carved covings.

"Oh, thank you my dear. Yes, I am a very lucky woman. *We've* been here for over thirty years now. It can be a bit draughty and a tad cold at times with over twenty rooms to heat, but *we* do love it. Anyway, that aside for the moment, you must call me Enid. Mrs Williams sounds so formal don't you think?"

We? Rebecca wondered.

"Thank you, Enid."

"I'm assuming these are from your previous employer, yes?"

"Oh, sorry Enid, yes they are. The reference is from dear Aunt Mae, my last employer," she replied as she feigned a dropped lip and wiped a false tear from her eye. Rebecca had deliberately not included her time spent in Wilf's employ.

"Oh, I'm sorry dear, I didn't mean to upset you, please forgive me. May I ask what happened to uh… your dear Aunt Mae?"

Pausing to reply and allowing enough time to remember her previously rehearsed answer, she retrieved the fabricated reference from the glass coffee table and slid it covertly back into her handbag.

"Well, Aunt Mae wasn't really my aunt you see, but she was my best friend and I loved her dearly," she said, dabbing her eyes. "Sadly, she passed away in her sleep and I'm having to deal with her daughter, Eliz-A-Beth. Although Aunt Mae and I were extremely close, she left me quite penniless and Eliz-A-Beth, who was very jealous of our close relationship, is now evicting me from the house. She also owes me two week's wages and is demanding that I leave immediately."

I do enjoy lying. It's so much fun.

"Well that's utterly disgraceful Rebecca," said Enid thoroughly convinced. "How awful, you must come and stay with us immediately my dear. I think it must have been fate or something, you know the way we bumped into each other in the corner shop the other day. I've always believed in fate. What's meant to be is meant to be Rebecca."

Like a wise old owl, she continued, "I must say I really did enjoy our little *tete-a-tete* afterwards. The funny thing is I was just about to advertise for a professional carer in our local newspaper, the *Bath Echo*. Well if I'm honest the advert was going to be for a lady companion, but no matter, because both title's amount to pretty much the same thing really don't, they? So, what a spot of luck us meeting like that. It's settled then. I'm assuming due to your current circumstances you would like to move in straightaway. Am I correct my dear?"

"Yes, you are. Oh, Enid that's so kind of you. I don't wish to sound rude or ungrateful but, before I accept your generous offer, may I ask what the terms are?"

Enid looked puzzled and took a few uncomfortable seconds to reply… "Oh, yes sorry dear, I understand. How silly of me, I know what you mean. In all the excitement I'd completely forgotten about the details. You mean the salary of course. The starting salary is twenty-five thousand per annum. All found that is."

"All found?" Rebecca asked, faking youthful naivety.

"Oh, sorry dear, it's my rather old-fashioned way of saying you'll receive your full salary, and your board, food and lodgings will be provided free of charge."

"I can't thank you enough Enid," replied a beaming Rebecca leaning across the table stroking the top of her frail wrinkled hand, enjoying the coldness of her diamond encrusted ring's scratching the bottom of her palm.

"Oh, you can thank me later Rebecca," she said, waving her hand like it was nothing. "There's one more thing I need to mention to you before you collect your belongings, and that is Archie."

"Archie?" asked Rebecca. *Archie must be the "we" then.*

"Yes Archie," Enid replied, wringing her hands nervously.

"Archie is my gardener, my handyman, my odd job man if you like, he's an absolute dear, you'll love him. Although he's been with me for over twenty-five years I must admit, and if

I'm perfectly honest with you, he can be a bit grumpy at times. Please try to ignore that though because underneath he's a real sweetheart."

"Oh, I can't wait to meet him. Does Archie live in?" Rebecca enquired, smiling sweetly.

"Live in? Oh, I see what you mean. Oh yes, Archie lives in. He keeps an eye on the place for me. Twenty years ago, he very cleverly installed the CCTV cameras you can see dotted around the place. He's also planning to install a burglar alarm later in the summer. I just let him get on with it. He knows all about that sort of thing being an ex-policeman and all that."

Ex-copper, cameras... shit, Archie could be a problem! Don't like cameras, do we? But no burglar alarm, so that's a plus. Okay, time to go Rebecca.

"Well, it's been delightful meeting you again. I can't thank you enough for the position Enid. I'll go and pack my things. What time is best for you Enid? What time would you like me to arrive?"

"Well, I do like to take a little nap in the afternoon, so shall we say around four my dear. Would four be okay?"

"Four's fine with me Enid, so I'll see you then."

Rebecca, at five-foot eight, towered over the hunched frame of this little old lady with her sickly-sweet smile and diamond encrusted rings. She performed an air kiss either side of her wrinkled cheeks.

"Can I smell Chanel?" Rebecca enquired.

"Yes, my dear, Chanel," Enid confirmed. "Nothing but the best at Lonsdale. I'll pick some up for you when we go shopping in Bath. Bye for now Rebecca and be careful it's really icy out there today."

"I will Enid. Bye, see you at four."

As the electric gates slid and scraped their way slowly across, out of the corner of her eye she could see a grey-haired man busily piling leaves into a wheelbarrow at the side of the big Edwardian mansion. He cast her a nod without offering a smile. She waved back at him smiling, but he looked away.

That must be dear sweet old Archie, Rebecca thought.

12. Rebecca

It was now seven long torturous weeks since Rebecca had joined Enid's employ as her *companion, carer* or whatever she liked to call it. It was early spring and every single hour of every day since she arrived at Lonsdale dear sweet old Enid Williams had run her ragged. Rebecca felt close to breaking point.

Fetch me this, will you? Nip down to the chemist, will you dear? Pass me that magazine over there, will you? Kiss my wrinkled ass Rebecca, will you? Oh, go on be a dear? And things weren't any better for "Dear sweet old Archie" as she insisted on calling the snooping suspicious twat. Oh, just run the mower over the back lawn, will you Archie? Oh, we're short of logs in the front lounge, fetch some in, will you? Be a dear.

Lonsdale was being run like a concentration camp, and its commandant just happened to be a sickly-sweet, wrinkled up old lady called Enid Williams. And she was a bloody tyrant. Rebecca had missed it at first but, with seven weeks under her belt, Enid was in full flow and Rebecca was right in the thick of it! *And Archie's isn't a sweet old dear at all. No, he's a grumpy old git who creeps around the halls at night listening at doors and staring through key holes. I suppose once a copper, always a bloody copper.*

Things were going from bad to worse for Rebecca now McDermott had *re-negotiated* the terms of their so-called *arrangement.* She was now going to receive exactly half of what she was getting before! And McDermott would happily pocket the rest. And that wasn't the worst of it because, out of her half, Rebecca had to pay her stepfather, Tom Thorneycroft.

So, something had to be done, and fast. Out of the twelve gold coins she'd stolen from Wilf, her share had been just four! And McDermott who'd fenced them had handed her just six thousand pounds in cash. So, in short, Rebecca was pissed right off. And rightly so.

I mean just look at him, my so-called stepfather that is. Okay, granted, he might furnish a few names here and there. But it's me that's doing all the hard work, shagging that bastard McDermott every time he clicks his fat little fingers. So, today Rebecca Thorneycroft is totally pissed off and I've had enough, something needs to change, either the pot gets bigger or one of those blood-sucking parasites has to go.

And I already know who that's going to be. But, how to do it? Now that's a totally different question, isn't it? It has to happen before we split the money. I can deal with McDermott afterwards. So there, you've answered your own question haven't you Rebecca? You need to kill that bastard of a stepfather of yours.

"Rebecccccca, are you upstairs dear?"

It's her again, she never stops.

"Yes Enid, I'll be down in a minute. I'm emptying your commode." *Stirring your shit… dear!*

"You won't be long, will you? I need you to walk me to the bank."

The bank, well that's a first.

"I'll be down in a couple of minutes. Get yourself ready and make sure you put a warm coat on. It's cold outside."

The tedium of walking her! She's so bloody slow. She shuffles along chatting to anyone stupid enough to offer even the slightest hint of a conversation. I've seen people cross the street and pull down their umbrellas just to get away from her.

126

"Morning Mr Fraser, how is poor Valerie…?" And it goes on, and on….

After an hour spent faffing around and constantly stop-starting, they eventually arrive at the bank just as the sun started to break through the cloudy sky above. The wind's up and blowing a gale down the tree-lined street as Rebecca helps Enid by taking her arm and negotiating the three stone steps leading into the bank.

It was a *Coutts Bank,* no less! *Nothing too good for good old Enid Williams is there?*

"A very good morning to you Mrs Williams. A trifle cold and blowy out there today but a lovely spring day all the same. How can I help you today?" was the gushing greeting and false smile from the grey-haired bank clerk sat on a stool the other side of the security screen. His badge said his name was Senior Bank Clerk, Victor Sheldon.

You're a bloody bank clerk, you pompous prick! thought Rebecca smiling courteously, her gesture largely ignored as the clerk looked away. *After all, who am I?* she thought. *I'm just the bloody carer.*

127

Enid placed the flat of her hands on the counter and moved her face closer to the screen, eyeing Sheldon up and down as one might a captured chimp at Bristol Zoo.

"A very good morning to you as well Mr Sheldon," she joyfully announced. "I would like to make my usual withdrawal, from my um… let me see… yes, my savings account if you don't mind."

Usual withdrawal? This sounds interesting.

"That's absolutely fine Mrs Williams," a smiling Sheldon confirmed while typing something into his state-of-the-art console. "I assume you're withdrawing the usual amount Mrs Williams?" he asked, leaning forward fixing his eyes on hers.

"You assume correctly Mr Sheldon," Enid confirmed, rifling through the disorganised mess inside her Chanel handbag as one of her statements fluttered to the floor. It was her savings account. Rebecca quickly bent down, picked it up and noted the amount in the bottom right-hand corner of the page.

"Here you are Enid," she said, handing it back to her face down and looking rather flushed as one might after discovering that your employer had over five hundred and eighty-seven thousand pounds. And that was just in her savings account!

"Thank you, Rebecca, I'm such an awful butter fingers these days. And yes, Mr Sheldon, I would like to withdraw the regular monthly amount of eight thousand in the usual denominations please."

Eight thousand! Fuck! thought Rebecca, as Sheldon offered the filthy-rich pensioner a condescending sickly-sweet smile through the glass and nodded politely as he replied, "Of course Mrs Williams, it's already been counted out for you. Give me a minute and I'll go and fetch it from the back." Then, lifting himself off his stool, he skipped off to the back.

"So," Rebecca asked, "That's an awful lot of money for you to be carrying around. Do you do this every month?" she tentatively enquired.

"Oh, yes dear, I've been doing this for well over a year now. I know it's a bit naughty of me," she whispered, as she sheepishly looked around the bank. "If I'm entirely honest with you, I've been trying to avoid paying those exorbitant death duties on my late husband Danny. I mean why should the tax man get it all Rebecca. Why should he? You tell me."

Enid held her tiny forefinger to her lips intimating secrecy before continuing. "You see, my dear Danny passed away a year ago last October and we'd been together for fifty-seven years. I was rather hoping we'd make the sixty, you know a letter from the Queen and all that, but sadly it wasn't to be. He was a bit of a character was my Danny boy, he was a retired bookmaker and dealt a little in… well un-cut diamonds you see. I shouldn't be telling you all this Rebecca, but I just feel that I can trust you somehow. I don't know what tells me that, but I can, can't I?"

"Of course, you can Enid," Rebecca replied, firmly giving a reassuring squeeze of Enid's cold hands.

"He absolutely despised paying taxes, so I suppose I have to abide by his wishes and make sure he pays as little as possible, especially now he's up there," she added, pointing at the sky and chuckling to herself like an over-spoilt seven-year-old child.

"I'm sorry Enid I only asked out of concern, you must miss him terribly?" said Rebecca, replying honestly for once and actually meaning it. A huge part of her wished she had her own "Danny boy", someone who would take care of her, someone she could rely on. Love even. But she couldn't because he simply didn't exist.

"Oh, yes I do dear," said Enid. "I miss him every single hour of every single day, but he's always with me right here by my side," she said dabbing her chalky white handkerchief drying her pale blue eyes, sniffing in an attempt to compose herself.

"You see Rebecca, Archie would normally accompany me to the bank, but he's feeling a bit under the weather today, so I've left him tucked up in bed with a hot toddy."

"How thoughtful of you Enid. You're so kind…" *Not!*

So, let me get this straight, you've been withdrawing eight grand every month for nigh on what? If it's just a year that would make it what? Do the maths Rebecca. Do the maths. Ninety-six grand! Plus, you might just have some diamonds stashed away as well. Bingo!

"I hope you've hidden it somewhere safe?" Rebecca tentatively probed, trying desperately hard not to arouse any suspicion.

But she had, and Enid's face tightened as she screwed her eyes and a previously unseen hardness crossed her tiny wrinkled face. And Rebecca quite rightly sensed that she'd overstepped the mark.

"There's no need for you to concern yourself with that, now is there Rebecca!" Enid snapped. "Where I keep my money and certain other things is my business and mine alone! I have a wonderful security system and only Archie and I know the combination to the safe. So, please you just concern yourself with getting me home nice and safe, okay dear."

Enid tapped Rebecca's arm, then her own nose intermating her rebuke at the unwanted prying on Rebecca's part. And Rebecca knew she'd been told.

Sheldon returned a few minutes later and slid a large brown envelope under the glass screen with its own gold *Coutts* logo printed in the top right-hand corner. Enid greedily stuffed it into her handbag as Rebecca looked at the ceiling without uttering another word.

"Thank you, Mr Sheldon, I'll see you next month God willing. Come on Rebecca, let's go, home, shall we? I fancy a nice game of Monopoly. Tell you what, you make the tea and bring the cake tray in and I'll set the board up. What do you say? After that you can light us a nice fire. Hey."

A little taken back following such a stern telling off Rebecca was purposely humble in her reply. "That sounds lovely Enid," she said, linking arms totally preoccupied with how she was going to get her hands on all that money. And Enid's latest revelation – the diamonds.

Rebecca entered the lounge and placed the first bucket of logs in the hearth as Enid sat in her chair busily counting out the Monopoly money and placing the chance cards in the centre lining up the red hotels and little green houses around the edge. Her *Chanel* handbag lay partially open to the side of her wing-backed armchair with the fat *Coutts* envelope tucked neatly inside. Rebecca could see the edges of the notes poking out all neatly folded over and staring invitingly back at her.

"It won't be long now Enid, we'll soon have this fire going," Rebecca said gleefully rubbing her hands together. "I'll go and fetch some more logs in, shall I?"

But Enid didn't reply and simply nodded in her general direction as she carried on counting out the money and assembling the board.

On her way back from the woodshed carrying the last two heavy buckets of logs, Rebecca passed the bay window in the lounge and noticed that the curtains had been pulled across, leaving a two-inch opening in the middle. She stopped and looked around to check nobody was about, placed the two brass scuttles down on the gravel path and bent down to sneak a quick look into the room, fully expecting to see Enid in her favourite armchair awaiting her return. But she wasn't. Instead she was standing at the far end of the lounge facing the bookcase holding three large books in her hands. And, as far as she could see, the manner in which she held them in both hands it looked as though they were attached somehow, almost as if they were glued together.

Then suddenly, without warning, Enid turned around and looked directly at the large bay window and, for a split second, appeared to be looking straight at Rebecca, causing her to instantly duck down. With her head tucked down below the frame she waited about thirty seconds before taking another look. This time Enid was sat down in her chair gently sipping the tea she'd made for her.

"Can I help you with those Rebecca?" came a loud thunderous voice from behind, causing her to take two steps back and almost jump out of her skin. She turned to find Archie standing there scratching the front of his green garden overalls, only a few feet away.

"Oh, Archie you gave me such a fright, I thought I…"

Archie didn't reply immediately. He stood for a few moments and looked her up and down suspiciously before responding.

"Sorry I didn't mean to frighten you Rebecca," he said. "But you were peering through Enid's window. Is… is something wrong?"

"No nothing's wrong at all Archie," Rebecca said, panting like a wet racehorse and holding her chest. "It's just the curtains were drawn, and I wondered if Enid was alright. I was on my way back with the logs when…."

"Don't fret Rebecca," Archie said, cutting her off with a wave of his arm, "No harm done. Tell you what let me carry those in for you. They look heavy."

"Thanks Archie, you're so kind." *No, you're not, you're a nosey, interfering old git. And why are you being so nice to me suddenly? Shit! I've messed this up!*

Rebecca ran on ahead and entered the lounge.

"Enid! Good news, Archie's here. He must be feeling better," she happily declared as Archie entered the room puffing and panting and placing the two heavy buckets in the middle of the hearth.

"Oh, nice to see you are up and about again Archie," Enid happily remarked. "Are you feeling better?" she asked, offering him one of her sickly-sweet smiles.

"Much better thanks Enid, just a head cold I think, nothing more," he said, gripping the end of his nose with his thumb and forefinger as if in confirmation.

"Good, so why don't you go up upstairs and relax. Take the weight off your feet Archie? I'm perfectly fine, Rebecca's just about to light us a nice fire and then we're going to start our game. Aren't we Rebecca?"

"Yes, Enid we are," answered Rebecca as Enid clapped her hands and Archie looked across the room staring straight at her. "So, the games afoot then Enid?" Archie said and Rebecca shivered…

13. Rebecca

Rebecca telephoned McDermott and Tom Thorneycroft early on Saturday morning to ask if they could meet her at the *Black Rook* pub at three o'clock the following day.

The *Black Rook* was a charming old village pub set in its own grounds just behind a fifteenth century church and was a regular haunt for locals of the village of Tormarton. Due to its remoteness, Rebecca felt that the chances of McDermott being seen drinking with a renowned dirty old villain like Tom Thorneycroft were, to say the least, extremely slim.

Intentionally leaving out any mention of the diamonds, she explained why she'd called the meeting and conveyed how she thought she may have stumbled across Enid's secret hiding place, where she kept her money. McDermott was all ears and unusually cheerful. Rebecca assumed it was probably due to the fact that up until that point he'd cleverly managed to distance himself from the sharp end of what he termed their *little arrangement.* In other words, she was the one taking all the risks and he was the one making all the profits.

Tom was frequently visiting the toilet and, if he wasn't in there, he'd be seen propping up the bar ordering another gin and tonic or demanding another beer. His pupils were heavily dilated, he was as high as a kite and it was blatantly obvious to Rebecca that he was flat out on cocaine, again. A couple of times she had to lean over the table telling him to "wipe that shit off his nose", only to be ignored or told to "Do one and mind your own fucking business".

McDermott was trying his best to ignore Tom's slurry and incoherent rantings, listening to Rebecca's description of the conversation she'd had with Enid during their walk back from the bank and how, when they'd arrived back at Lonsdale, she'd seen Enid standing at the far end of the lounge holding three large books in her hands. It seemed obvious that must be where the safe is located and where her money was hidden. And if they are able to find out the combination to the safe, the rest would be easy, and they'd be home and dry.

For the first time since they'd met, McDermott just listened rather than holding court like some despotic dictator. Rebecca felt a semblance of control entering their normally tumultuous relationship. Whether it was intended or not, McDermott was displaying a level of respect she hadn't experienced before.

Eventually Tom returned from yet another one of his visits to the gents, fell into the chair opposite her and the conversation stalled. Rebecca was close to breaking point. Tom Thorneycroft was slowly, but very surely, pushing her over the edge. Something needed to be done. And it had to be quick.

Clearly irritated, McDermott told him to "shut up!" on several occasions, but Tom ignored him and continued happily babbling away to himself, completely ignorant and oblivious to their public surroundings.

Once more Tom headed for the toilet and McDermott sighed shaking his head in resignation as Rebecca continued to explain.

"The safe has to be in the bookcase," she said. "It's got to be hidden behind those books. She's been withdrawing eight grand every month for nigh on a year now. What on earth can she be spending it on? I mean my wages are transferred directly into the bank every month, so it's not for my benefit. I suppose there's always a chance she might be paying Archie in cash. I don't know! But I do know this. He isn't on two grand a bloody week, is he?"

"She has to be hoarding it," Rebecca confidently announced as McDermott slid further forward in his chair deep in thought.

"At the bank Enid let it slip that this dead husband of hers used to be a bookmaker. Apparently, he was a bit of a lad in his day and since he passed away, she's been trying to avoid paying death duties. God only knows how much is in the safe. Your guess is as good as mine. But if it's eight grand a month for a year that would make it ninety-six grand, wouldn't it?"

Tom returned from the toilet and his eyes lit up as he heard the last part of the conversation. Rebecca could sense his drug-infested brain muddling through the maths.

"You know anything about safes then Tommy boy?" McDermott asked him smirking, perfectly aware that the question was completely rhetorical. But even in that state Tom Thorneycroft couldn't resist a brag, even to a copper like McDermott. So, he tapped his nose and slurred through his reply.

"There ain't nuffin old Tommy Thorneycroft here don't know about safes. You just get me in the place, and I'll blow the bloody…"

"Keep your fucking voice down!" McDermott said angrily, cutting him off and glancing round to see if anybody could hear. "We don't want the whole fucking pub to know you wanker! And we don't want the place blown sky high either you idiot! Rebecca's on to something here. This has got to look like an inside job. If it's a burglary, it gets really bloody complicated. Forensics will be all over it and believe me nobody wants that. So, inside job it is. What's the name of the gardener again?"

"Archie," replied Rebecca, watching a snarling Tom swaying backwards and forwards in his chair. "He's the one who originally installed the security system."

McDermott seemed to like that, clearly a plan was forming. "So, the chances are he also knows the combination to the safe then yeah?" McDermott asked.

"Of course, he does, Enid told me he does," Rebecca confirmed. "It's only the two of them that know it."

McDermott clicked his thumb and forefinger together. "Good because that tiny piece of information just made this whole thing that much easier."

"How? Why?" she asked confused. "He isn't going to write it down for me, is he?" she said. "And before you ask. No! I'm not shagging him."

"No, you're missing the point. Enid obviously trusts this Archie, so all you need to do is find the make and model of the safe and the rest's a doddle. You see, all safe manufacturers have a master combination, a sort of override code, just in case some old twat like Enid locks herself out or forgets the combination."

"It happens all the time, especially with the rise of dementia, so once you get the make and model the rest should be a piece of cake. Just as luck would have it, these master combinations are stored on police computers. If Archie is the only one in the house, apart from Enid, who knows the combination, then bingo! It'll look like he nicked it."

McDermott sat back in his chair and folded his arms like someone who'd just discovered penicillin, rather than a bent copper planning to stitch up a vulnerable old lady.

"What about the cameras?" Rebecca asked, "They're everywhere, it's like the Big Brother house in there."

"But…" Tom said.

"But nothing," McDermott said, cutting him short as he leant forward and returned his attention to Rebecca.

"Well, before we rush in, we need to know if it's a recordable system, that's really important. We'll also need to know the location of the mains electrical switch. If we need to organise a power outage it could take months. Failing that Rebecca, you'll need to trip the main fuse at the box."

McDermott snapped his fingers again before confidently adding, "And Bob's your uncle."

"I think I need another beer," said a clearly disinterested Tom as he pushed himself out of the chair and staggered over to the bar.

"We've got to do something about him and quick Rebecca," said McDermott watching as he tossed his loose change across the counter, demanding another pint.

"That's the first time we've ever agreed on anything McDermott," Rebecca replied, looking across at the bedraggled sight of her drugged up, drunken stepfather relying heavily on the bar.

"So, what do you suggest?" she asked him, already knowing the answer.

McDermott smiled. The look in his eyes explained everything as he took another sip of his drink.

"Well, I could always get him locked up on some trumped-up charge," he said. "But that would be too easy wouldn't it? My guess is that as soon as he's banged up, he'll drop us in it and sing like a canary. So that only leaves us with one alternative, doesn't it Rebecca? And I think we both know what that is, don't we?" he asked, placing his empty beer glass on the table.

By now, Tom was involved in a heated row with the barman who'd had the audacity to refuse him another drink and his rantings were loud enough to be heard by everyone.

"Come on Rebecca, let's get out of here," McDermott said getting up, "Before it really kicks off and that barman calls the old bill. He's completely out of control."

Rebecca simply nodded in agreement, grabbed her handbag and followed him out. Tom didn't even notice them leaving as by then he was pinned to the bar by a large bald-headed man threatening to "Punch his bloody lights out."

After a short walk to the end of the scenic old village, they entered the *Fox & Hounds*. Rebecca sat down at a small table while McDermott went to the bar to order her a large gin and tonic, and a pint.

Rebecca glanced around at the scattering of locals in the quaint little bar. She noticed an old couple happily feeding coin after coin into a battered old fruit machine sipping what appeared to be two bitter lemons. The scene, the peaceful atmosphere, was in total contrast to the one they'd left behind.

"So, Rebecca, what do you suggest?" McDermott asked as he returned with the drinks. "Tell me what you want me to do about Tommy bloody Thorneycroft?"

He already knew the answer, but he wanted Rebecca to say it first as he took a long lingering mouthful of his pint swirling the amber liquid around in his mouth. His eyes still unable to make their mind up if they preferred her tits or her thighs.

"He has to go," was all Rebecca could say. Before taking a sip of her drink and adding, "He means nothing to me. He's a complete bastard and I've had enough."

Strangely, and unintentionally, she felt a moistness forming in the corners of her eyes. She sat for a few moments deep in thought then, from somewhere and she wasn't sure where, she plucked up enough courage to confess for the very first time the most utterly distressing and awful period of her life. And to a person she despised and hated.

"He abused me, you know that don't you, when I was little," her forthright and candid admission betrayed an inner sadness as a feeling of unjustified shame swept over her.

"I must have been about ten when it started," she said, dabbing her eyes with a tissue. "So, yes, go ahead and kill the bastard. I want this to be over. I need to start living my life."

"Yeah, I will. And yes Rebecca, I'd guessed that," said McDermott, looking down at the carpet in an attempt to mask his own shame for what he'd done to her.

"Okay, it's time he went! I'll take care of it. Leave him to me," he added, but continued looking down.

Rebecca wasn't listening. She was lost in the cold, dark walls of her own nightmare. *I can't believe I'm just calmly ordering his death. But he deserves it, doesn't he? He's a monster, he's turned me into a monster. So, go on do it. Kill the bastard.*

Rebecca looked McDermott straight in the eyes. "Despite what he's done, I don't want him to feel anything. No pain… It has to be quick; you know sort of…"

"He won't feel a thing," McDermott assured her, lying through his teeth. "They'll simply drag an old drunk out of the River Avon in a couple of days and this will be all over."

Rebecca shuddered at the sheer coldness of his callous response, making it sound like an everyday event.

"Good, so we're agreed then Rebecca," McDermott said as he reached out and held her trembling hand in his.

"Call me Andy, will you?" he asked, softly stroking the top of her bitterly cold hands. But she wasn't listening, she was miles away, lost to a world only she could enter.

I don't have a choice, do I? she thought, staring into space. *It's only a matter of time before he gets picked up paralytic somewhere and starts babbling. McDermott might be a bastard, but he's right this time. He has to go!*

She looked down and noticed McDermott stroking her hand. She pushed him away and replied, using just a single word. "Agreed." And in a conversation that lasted less than half an hour, Tom Thorneycroft's fate was sealed.

"Please call me Andy, Rebecca, McDermott asked again.

"I know I've been a bastard and I truly am sorry. But I do have feelings for you and I'm really enjoying our little arrangement."

I bet you are, you blackmailing Bastard!

So, back to my place then is it? I've just bought a new flat up on the Downs. I reckon you'll love it, especially the view from the bedroom." McDermott thought that was comical and laughed.

But Rebecca didn't…

14. Rebecca

Saturdays were purgatory for Rebecca. Enid insisted she back combed her hair as she read aloud the front-page headlines from the *Bath Echo*.

"Look at this Rebecca. It says here that an unidentified man has been found floating in the River Avon. His body was discovered in the early hours of yesterday morning. A member of the public telephoned the emergency services after they saw a body trapped between the stanchions, just below Bristol Bridge."

"The police are treating the incident as non-suspicious at this stage and are calling for any witnesses to the incident to come forward. They think it may have occurred in the early hours of Thursday morning. How dreadful Rebecca! The poor man must have been drunk, then fell in the river and drowned? What do you think?"

Fuck! That's quick, he's gone!

The sudden news overwhelmed Rebecca. She was in shock. It was too soon. She was rooted to the spot for a moment, gripping the hairbrush tightly in her hand and staring over Enid's shoulder at the headlines.

"Can you excuse me Enid," she asked, clasping her hand across her mouth in disbelief. "I feel a bit queasy. I think I need to visit the loo."

"Yes of course my dear," Enid replied and without reaction she turned her attention to the back page and the day's horseracing in Bath.

Locking the toilet door and leaning her body against the coldness of the tiled wall, she stared into the mirror and asked herself, "What are you crying for, you idiot! McDermott said he'd take care of it! And he has, hasn't he? Stop your whinging, tears are no good to you now. You should be glad he's gone. You're finally rid of the bastard."

She continued talking to her reflection, "it's too soon, I'm just not ready," she said quietly, as she slid down the wall onto the floor and suddenly realised that she was now all alone in the world. Tom was her only link to the past and, no matter how dreadful or how terrifying that past had been, it was hers, only hers.

After lying on the floor a few minutes, she heard a loud *knock* on the door, and she could hear Enid outside.

"Rebecca, Rebecca… are you okay in there? Are you all right my dear, do you need anything?" Enid asked, pressing her ear to the door.

"I'm fine Enid, thank you, I'm not feeling very well that's all. Bad stomach, I think. Don't worry, I'll be out in a minute."

Enid's voice seemed to calm a little after that. "Okay, as long as you're all right, Archie and I are going to take a stroll down to the bank, we won't be long. If you're well enough later, would you run a vacuum over the ground floor reception and the lounge. There are bits everywhere. But, of course, only if you're feeling better my dear?"

Rebecca could sense her ear to the door, the sound of her heavy breathing reminding her of an old fairy-tale from the past. The one where three little piglets are trapped inside a house and a wolf is threatening to huff and puff and blow the door down. She could sense Enid's face straining at the door as she waited for her to reply.

"No, no that's fine Enid, just leave it to me. I'll see to it as soon as I'm feeling better."

"Okay dear, see you later, and I do hope you feel better."

The conversation ended there. Rebecca listened at the door as Enid spoke to Archie as they shuffled off.

"Come on Archie, we'll grab a nice milky coffee and a custard tart at the bakery on the corner. Link up old friend, link up."

A few minutes later, the front door slammed shut. And at last she had the house to herself.

I need my bloody mobile… where's my mobile…? I've left it in the bedroom.

Rebecca pulled the bolt back, rushed out of the bathroom and took a quick look through the opaque glass of the front door. She could see two silhouettes walking down the path. So, running up two flights of stairs like a bomb had gone off, she snatched the mobile off the top of her bed and from memory whispered out the numbers as she dialled. A couple of seconds later, her call was answered.

"Hello, Detective Sergeant Andrew McDermott speaking, Avon and Somerset Constabulary. How can I help you?"

"It's me… It's Rebecca."

There was a short pause before he replied… "No, I don't want bloody PPI! And stop calling me on this number! In fact, take it off your friggin database will you!"

The line went dead.

She assumed that was code for he'll call me back when he's free, he must be with someone.

She pushed the off button and returned downstairs, glancing at her watch while she worked the numbers.

They've been gone what… five minutes already, say another ten to walk to the bank, then they'll probably spend another twenty minutes in the café and probably another five spent jabbering to some poor old soul she's managed to corner on the street. Add another ten to walk back and that makes fifty minutes in total.

Shit, bollocks! The cameras!

Almost immediately, she gripped her stomach feigning a sudden pain and bent over double as she staggered underneath the watchful eyes of the camera in the hallway. The red tell-tale light was flashing as she slowly walked towards the hallway cupboard to where the vacuum was kept.

Then regaining her upright posture and adding to her near-perfect act by wiping her forehead with the palm of her hand, she opened the cupboard door and lifted the heavy Kirby out, while also stealing a quick look at the antiquated fuse board on the shelf just above her head. The old video recorder was on another shelf just above and to the side was the main switch. Her performance was flawless, or so she thought as she closed the cupboard door and entered the lounge.

As she was uncoiling the long flexible cable from the vacuum handle, her phone rang. It was McDermott. She walked into the hall to answer it.

"Hello," she said, walking towards the back of the hall and attempting to keep out of sight of the camera.

"What's up?" came the reply, his voice sounded distant and strangely echoey.

"So, he's dead then?" she asked, rubbing her eyes.

"Yeah," McDermott replied, sighing… "I'm sorry."

"No, you're not!" she responded angrily.

"Look Rebecca, I haven't got time for this right now, so please just tell me what you want!"

"I think I've found a way to turn the cameras off."

The line was silent for a few seconds and she could hear a sound like dripping water in the background.

"What's that noise?" she asked.

"It's a dripping tap. I'm sat on the crapper up on the Downs. Now hurry up and get on with it. What's the plan?"

A picture of McDermott sat with his trousers down around his ankles quickly rushed through her mind and she started to feel sick. But, swallowing hard, she was able to answer.

"The main switch is in the cupboard by the front door. I'll be able to turn it off when I put the vacuum back in the cupboard, you know sort of accidentally knock the switch."

"Good! Now listen, is it an old system? What type of video recorder is it?"

"Looks to me like a really old Betamax."

"Good, then we're laughing."

Laughing… I'm not laughing.

"Right, while you're putting the vacuum away, knock off the main switch, then check the light's out on the hall camera before you have a look at the safe. Your best bet is to photograph it on your mobile. But whatever happens don't send it to me on this phone. Keep hold of it till we meet up, okay. Now, by knocking out the main switch, everything will go off – the electric alarm clocks, the DVD player, everything in the house. So, when you're with Enid later, make sure you tell her you knocked it off accidentally as you were putting the vacuum away. Remember… that's essential Rebecca, have you got that?"

"Yes, yes, it was my idea in the fucking first place! I'm not stupid you know. I've got it," she replied, fed up to the back teeth with his lecture. "Look, I need to vacuum now, so I'll call you a bit later, bye."

She checked her watch and noted that there was exactly twenty minutes left. She switched on the vacuum and began to run it up and down the lounge, while also holding her stomach and being careful not to pay any attention to the bookshelf.

Ten minutes later, she was done. *I'll tell Enid I felt too ill to do the rest*, she thought, as she coiled up the lead and returned the heavy Kirby back into the bottom of the cupboard. Just as she was closing the door, she *accidently* tripped over the bottom door frame.

Hidden from sight of the hall camera, she reached and pushed the main switch up. Everything electrical in the house instantly died. Time seemed to stand still as the whole house fell silent. She checked the camera light was off and once more returned to the lounge to take a peek out from behind the curtains.

The street was deserted, and everything was quiet outside. She walked across to the bookshelf, stopped for a moment and looked up at the hundreds of books on the five shelves. She recalled that Enid hadn't used a ladder that day and she had stood somewhere near the middle. She ran her tiny fingers along the middle row and started to pull on each book individually. They all moved independently of the others, that is until she reached a book entitled *War and Peace* written by somebody called *Leo Tolstoy* which felt denser and sort of heavier than the others. As she very gently pulled it out towards her, she noticed two other books were attached to it.

Placing them down on the carpet, she stood and looked through the tunnel left by the missing books. Right at the back she could see a shiny aluminium safe with a black dial on the front and the words *El Diablo Security* etched across its front. She removed her iPhone from her pocket, funnelled her arm through the gap and pressed the camera button twice. A loud crashing noise from outside startled her. She quickly replaced the books and ran over to the lounge window.

There was a whole commotion going on. A car had backed into the rear of another and she could see Enid and Archie standing the other side of the electric gates happily watching as both drivers confronted one another. Then, less than a second later with his arm still firmly entwined, Archie turned to stare inquisitively towards the house. From that distance he couldn't see Rebecca hidden behind the curtains, but she ducked anyway and began to crawl along beneath the windowsill.

Reaching the hall, she got to her feet, opened the cupboard door and pulled the trip switch down to the *on* position. She could hear the dull *humming* noise of the electric gate motors from outside, as they slowly slid across.

Stop shaking Rebecca. Pull yourself together and try to act normally.

Two dark shadows gradually filled the opaque glass of the front door as she stood listening to the key turning in the lock. Taking two steps back, she held her breath as Archie followed by Enid walked in.

"Good God Rebecca! You look like you've seen a ghost," Archie declared looking her up and down. "You're as white as a sheet girl, are you that bad?" he asked, guiding Enid through the opening.

Rebecca held her hand to her mouth as she started to confess. "I'm sorry, while you were out, I put the Kirby in the cupboard, had a funny turn and stupidly tripped over that bloody door frame at the bottom," Rebecca said, pointing towards it.

"I tried to stop myself falling headfirst into the cupboard and as I reached out for something to grab hold of, I accidently tripped out the main fuse. I've re-set it now so no harm done. It was only off for a few minutes."

That should sort out the time difference… she hoped.

Archie didn't utter a single word. Instead he opened the cupboard door and looked straight up towards the video recorder to check the red was light was on. He then wiggled the main switch using his thumb and forefinger.

"Never mind no harm done Enid," Archie said, "It does that now and again, the wiring needs replacing."

Rebecca didn't notice any hint of suspicion in his tone and Enid wasn't really listening, seemingly much more concerned with offering Rebecca one of those sickly smiles of hers.

"Are you still feeling under the weather Rebecca?" she asked.

"Yes," Rebecca replied, "it's my stomach, I must have picked up a tummy bug or something. I hope you don't catch it. Would you mind terribly if I took the rest of the day off? I think I'll pop down to the chemist and see if they can give me something to help."

Enid stood deep in thought as her pet hate was being alone. *I've got Archie*, she thought to herself and readily agreed.

"No, no, of course not Rebecca. You go off and get yourself something from the chemist. You're right, I can't afford to catch something at my age, can I Archie?" she said, tugging his arm as she led him into the lounge. But Archie didn't reply and didn't look at Rebecca…

15. Archie

Very little was known about Archibald Reginald Cunningham, prior to him joining Enid's staff as a gardener and general handyman twenty-five years ago. At the time his *curriculum vitae* said that, after being discharged from the British army with a good conduct medal and a mention in dispatches, Archie had spent the following three years as an Inspector in the Royal Hong Kong police force before transferring back to the Met, with the reduced rank of Detective Sergeant.

Enid and her late husband, Danny, had asked Archie the reason behind his reduction in rank and he had provided an honest and candid answer, pointing out that all Colonial ranks were automatically reduced by a factor of one when returning to what he termed the *Motherland.*

So, Archie was employed there and then, on the spot so to speak, and his first assignment was to install a state-of-the-art camera security system. He read all the manuals and books he could get his hands on and, much to Enid and Danny's delight, set about his new task like a man possessed.

Consequently, Archie knew precisely where every switch, camera and wire were located. More importantly, he knew the system he'd installed all those years before didn't have a back-up recording system. And he wondered if Rebecca might be aware of that. Even now, at the age of 77, he still had a natural instinct for seeing people for what they really were. He couldn't describe it or put it into words, but it was like a sort of itch he couldn't scratch. And Rebecca certainly made him itch.

So, ejecting the large video tape from the hallway machine and stuffing it into his jacket pocket, he walked across the highly manicured lawns towards his tool shed set at the rear of the big Georgian house. His shed was just beneath a weeping willow tree and it was where all those years before Archie had terminated all of the mains data cabling and installed his own portable *Betamax* tape recorder.

Archie pushed the video tape into the slot, pressed the play button on the console down firmly and waited for a moment naturally expecting the machine to *click* and *whirl* its way to the start position. But nothing happened. He sat blankly staring at the screen before remembering that he'd wired the main switch in the hall to a secret override button installed below his workbench.

As he flicked the old Bakelite switch to the *on* position, the machine instantly omitted a loud *whirring* noise as it sprung to life and the tape began to rewind. Archie had complete control of the system from one central point, and Archie liked nothing more than being in control. The greenish greyish screen flickered to life as the tape stopped and rewound itself omitting a loud *clunk*! The screen froze at the point where Enid had been talking to Rebecca through the closed bathroom door. He pushed the fast-forward button, followed by the play button. And, although grainy in its monochrome format, he was able to make out Rebecca emerging from the toilet less than a minute after he and Enid had left the house.

He watched as she looked across at the front door and a few seconds later she dashed up the stairs like a woman possessed.

"Thought you were meant to be ill Rebecca?" Archie whispered to himself.

Less than a minute later she was walking back down the stairs and this time she was holding her stomach. Her movements much slower, more laboured somehow. The *act* reminding him of his son when he used to fake stomach pains when trying to bunk off school.

Archie pressed the pause button, pushed his bi-focal glasses further up his nose and moved his face closer to the screen, glaring at the grainy black and white image of Rebecca.

"Did you just look up at the hall camera Rebecca?" he asked himself. "Well did you? Because I'd bet my police pension you did."

He pushed the play button, watching as she walked along the hallway towards the hall cupboard, still holding her stomach. But still her movements seemed wooden, enacted somehow. So, as far as Archie was concerned, it was a performance for the benefit of the cameras, beyond obvious that she knew she was being watched.

She opened the cupboard door, removed the vacuum cleaner, placed it down on the carpet and then wheeled it into the lounge. As she began uncoiling the cable from the handle she suddenly stopped, looked down at something and pulled her phone out of her apron pocket.

"Human instinct, big mistake that girl," Archie whispered chuckling to himself. "Bloody amateurs."

Possibly aware of her mistake, but now holding the phone to her ear, she walked back towards the hall with her left hand held casually on her hip, her jet-black hair passing just below the camera lens. She was now out of sight. Just like she'd planned.

"Hiding now Rebecca, are we?" he said under his breath. "That's your second mistake girl."

The timer on the screen's top right-hand corner told him that three minutes and twenty seconds had elapsed since she'd pulled the vacuum out and entered the lounge. *Three minutes and twenty seconds*, he thought.

Then, just as it was designed, the screen froze as the motion detector switched from the hall to the lounge and Rebecca was now running the Kirby across the lounge carpet, very cleverly still holding her stomach as she pushed it backwards and forwards.

"All part of the act Rebecca. You can't kid a kidder."

Sensing the tape was about to end, Archie pressed the half speed button and watched in slow motion as she coiled the flexible cord around the upright steel cylinder, walk back and return it to the bottom of the cupboard.

His view was obstructed for a few seconds as she opened the cupboard door. Then all of a sudden there was nothing. He was just looking at a blank screen with a few static noise lines running across it. A couple of seconds later the screen sprung to life again and Archie could see Enid and himself talking to Rebecca in the hallway, following their return from the bank.

He pressed the pause button and a frozen grainy image of Rebecca stared straight back at him from the darkness of the shed. Aided by the on-screen timer, he quickly did the maths and worked out that the system had been down for a full four minutes and twenty-eight seconds.

Four minutes and twenty-eight seconds, he thought, stroking his chin. *More than enough time to re-set a trip switch. So, what are you really up to then Rebecca…?*

16. Stephan

Finishing his conversation with Rebecca, McDermott stuffed the iPhone back into his jacket pocket and opened the door to the filthy cubicle. As he began washing his hands and looking up at the battered old stainless-steel wall mirror, there a was reflection of a man wearing a black hoody staring straight back at him.

"You, uh, looking for something mate?" the man asked in a broad Bristolian accent. "You wanna buy some double O, or crack cocaine maybe, weed, sex, even…?"

Without looking up and shaking his wet hands in the sink, McDermott spun round, grabbed the man by the hood, slammed his body into the inflexible hardness of the toilet wall and bent his arm painfully up his back. He screamed out in agony, "Please mate, don't hurt me! I was just…"

"Shut it! You piece of shit! I'm old bill you wanker! Look, fucking warrant card mush," McDermott shouted, scraping the sharp laminated card across the man's face.

"I don't want any trouble geez! Just trying to make a livin', that's all. Give us a break mate, will ya!"

The very last thing McDermott needed at that moment was more damn paperwork. He hadn't arrested a street dealer in years. He had bigger fish to fry. But still he increased his grip and yanking the man's head down and forcing his arm further up his back, he screamed out again in agony.

McDermott placed his mouth to the man's ear and whispered a simple question, "How long you been in here, ah? Come on, tell me! How long?"

"I only just got ere mate. I just got here. Let me go mate, I didn't hear nuffin', nuffin'."

McDermott stopped to think for a second. *If he's telling me the truth, I'm in the clear. If he isn't, who'd believe the word of a down-and-out piece of shit like him.*

"Good, now fuck off before I nick you," he said, swinging the man round to face him. "And don't forget I'll recognise that face of yours anywhere, especially with that nice little scar of yours… geez."

Later that night, Stephan Earl entered the strobing lights and seedy atmosphere of his favourite haunt, *La Toya* nightclub, set on one of the side streets just behind Bristol City centre at the bottom of the old Gloucester Road.

As far as Stephan was concerned, entering the *La Toya* was like attending his own personal trade fair. People quite literally lined the dingy corridors and toilets as they anticipated his arrival. The music was a mixture of reggae and soul, but Stephan couldn't really identify because his hearing was -004 negative, a problem he'd had since early childhood. He could hear peoples' voices easily enough, especially those standing near to him, but the music all sounded the same. He'd never told anyone or sought help for the condition. His mother knew, but she was long gone.

Stephan approached the bar and ordered his usual rum and coke, stacked high with plenty of ice just as he liked it. He was sweating, his right arm ached like hell and he felt for the plaster on his right cheek following his earlier encounter with the *old bill* in the toilet. The barman, a Caucasian that Stephan suspected was gay and who went by the name of *Antoine*, served him. Antoine knew Stephan as the youngest of the Earls, the toughest family in the community that made up St Augustine's.

Stephan Elias Earl for a moment stood looking around as he surveyed his seedy empire, his face still retaining that cocky arrogance that it always had. He needed a lift, another line. As he was walking towards the toilets at the side of the dance floor, he heard a voice calling out from behind, "Steph, Steph!"

He turned around and squinted, trying to recognise the face through the club's strobing lights. He was aware it was a girl's voice and then he realised – it was Amanda.

"Hey girl, how you doin' babe?" he asked, as she walked over towards him.

Amanda, Stephan's ex-girlfriend, stood a good two inches taller than him and, with blonde hair, long legs and an ass to die for, was well sought after. But tonight, like every other night since the spilt, Amanda was completely out of her face on a cocktail of cocaine, alcohol and skunk. Stephan had humped her six ways from Sunday in every position known to man during the whole of their three-month relationship, and that was partially the reason she'd dumped him, his appetite for sex and hard drugs preceded him.

Stephan looked her up and down, rolling his tongue and secretly wishing he could take her again. In the two months they'd been a so-called *item*, Stephan had happily introduced her to crack cocaine and all sorts of class 'A' drugs. Then, right at the end of their tumultuous relationship, he'd very kindly placed a syringe and a gram of heroin in her tiny hand. So, in short bless her, Amanda was now well and truly hooked.

Bill Blake, Amanda's father, a retired and extremely well-respected ex-Tory councillor had warned her years ago about the dangers of taking hard drugs. But she'd lied to him like she always had, telling him that she'd seen the light now and whatever happened she would never touch drugs again.

In the end, none of it mattered and she just carried on regardless because by then it was too late, she was already lost to the madness.

"Great to see you again Mand, you look fantastic," Stephan said, characteristically lying through his pearly white teeth.

Amanda had heard Stephan's chat up line thousands of times before and, even after what he'd put her through, she still liked him. She'd even admit he was capable of a little kindness at times, but only if you caught him in the right mood. Sadly, deep down, Amanda craved just one thing – a quick fix – and it was only Stephan who could provide her with that. All the signs were there – thinning features, teeth that hadn't seen a toothbrush in a while, a wanton exhaustive desperation in her eyes – and that's exactly what made her such easy prey for a *businessman* like Stephan Elias Earl.

"Come on and join us Stephan," Amanda said, "We're sat over there at the long bar. I'm with Kate, you remember Kate?" she asked nervously grimacing.

Stephan remembered Kate all right, *the interfering bitch*, he thought as he looked around the club. Ii was close to empty. A few bar props were scattered here and there, but not enough for a good night's business. So, he decided to take her up on the invitation and said, "Lead the way Mand," with an outstretched hand, knowing full well she hated being called *Mand*. Stephan followed from behind and cheekily winked at Kate as he arrived at the bar.

"So, what's going on then, Mand?" he asked her. "You met anyone yet? If you haven't, I've got something in here that'll brighten your night up, for the right price of course?"

Stephan reached into his pocket and held up a small plastic envelope with a red devil logo printed on the front. He flapped it less than an inch from her face as she swallowed hard trying to ignore his tempting offer.

"If you want to know, Stephan, I'm still waiting for Mr Right to come along. You know me, never happy," she replied, faking a sort of inner happiness. She was hot. Sweat beads were running down her face. She was way past desperate. So, there and then, she decided to ask him outright.

"So, what's the price this time then Stephan?" she asked, already guessing the answer.

"Well Mand, my pockets are bulging babe! But it's gonna cost you. You know me girl, nothing for nothing."

Amanda knew exactly what he wanted. So, as the sweat made her eyes sting, she faked another smile and took another sip of her drink. She asked herself, *what the fuck?*

"Okay Stephan, you've got me. You win, quick fuck or a blow job around the back and that'll cost you a gram, okay."

"Suits me fine Mand," Stephan replied, clearly satisfied as he placed his drink down on the bar casting a cheeky wink at Kate asking her to "Keep an eye on that for me will you darlin? This won't take long."

Kate didn't reply. Instead she looked away and shook her head in disgust. She despised Stephan Earl and everything he stood for. His infamous reputation for supplying hard drugs to the patrons of *La Toya* infuriated her. A seething Kate watched as Amanda stood up noisily, scraped her stool across the marble floor, then hand in hand walked out with him.

Half an hour later, Amanda and Stephan ambled back into the club and she stood next to Kate pulling on strands of her long blonde hair. Some powdery white remnants of her recent fix still deposited on the end of her nose.

"Wipe that shit off your nose, will you!" shouted Kate, looking around the club. "Why do you make it look so bloody obvious?"

"Ooooh… sorry Kate, fancy a line, do we?" Amanda replied provocatively, pinching the end of her nose.

"No, I bloody don't! Why do you do this to yourself? You've got everything going for you! Nice mum, plenty of money. For fuck's sake, get a grip! And… dump that prick once and for all!"

Kate, hopping mad, turned her back and took a sip of her drink. She waited for Amanda's response. And it wasn't long in coming as Amanda spun her around and started shouting two inches from her face.

"Why don't you just fuck off and mind your own business, fucking coppers daughter!"

But Kate wasn't fazed. She simply rolled her eyes in disgust as she turned her unwanted attention towards Stephan, plunging her finger deep into his chest. "Tell you what maggot!" she snarled, "Why don't you piss off and leave her alone. Just look at the state she's in. My dad could order a raid on this place just like that," Kate said, clicking her fingers an inch from his face. "She's my best friend, and you're not going to fuck her life up. You got that!"

Although more than a physical match for Kate, Stephan hated confrontations, especially public ones. Embarrassing rows were bad for business, so he just turned to grin confidently at Amanda and asked her if she "Fancied another line?"

Amanda stood thinking for a moment before looking at Kate who, by now, was mentally pleading with her to say "No!" But it was less than hopeless and instead she simply nodded at Stephan who grabbed her by the hand and both of them walked towards the exit.

As the night wore on, it became glaringly obvious that her friend was completely lost to the drugs. She watched Amanda from across the other side of the club begging Stephan for yet another bag. His reaction was to laugh in her face as she pleaded with him for another fix.

"Please… Amanda slow down," Kate begged as she walked over and held her arm. "I haven't seen you all night! You're either up there on the dance floor making a twat of yourself, or you're outside shagging that prick Stephan."

Amanda just stared at her friend with a blank expression. She felt judged and felt she'd had enough of Kate and her boring, repetitive lectures and, like most addicts, all she wanted to do was share her awful addiction. Time after time, she'd tried to introduce Kate to the seedy dark world of hard drugs and failed. So, she simply put her finger to her lips and made a *shushing* sound before slurring through her reply.

"There's something I need to tell you Kate", she whispered into her ear giggling. "And believe me, you ain't gonna like it."

Then, without another word, she walked towards the dance floor to see if she could scrounge a line from one of Stephan's paying customers. Kate was furious and far from satisfied. She wanted answers. *What the hell does that mean? You ain't gonna like it?*

She followed Amanda to the edge of the dance floor, grabbed her by the arm and swivelled her around. Amanda was having none of it. She simply repeated her previous statement.

"I'll tell you later, but you're not gonna like it Kate, I can promise you that. It's really bloody interesting you being a miss high and mighty copper's daughter and all that."

Kate tightened her grip on Amanda's arm demanding that she tell her now, but Amanda just shrugged her off calmly, "Later Kate, you'll just have to wait."

Kate released her grip and watched as Amanda staggered on to the dance floor. Stephan had cast her aside hours before when she'd run out of money and traded her in like a second-hand car after coming across, yet another drugged up drunken female passed out in the ladies' toilets.

Later that evening, in a taxi on the way towards the leafy suburb of Downend, Amanda insisted on alternating between singing at the top of her voice or taking great lunging gulps from a hidden wine bottle. Twice the driver had to tell her to "Shut up and put that bottle away!" And twice she chose to ignore him.

"So, Amanda," Kate asked, "What is it you so desperately wanted to tell me in the club? Me being a spoilt little 'copper's daughter' and all that," emphasising the word *copper*.

Amanda smirked, taking another lunging gulp from the wine bottle before starting to tell her.

"Well you're not going like this Kate, so don't kill the messenger. I consider us good friends, so I think you have a right to know. Anyway, a couple of hours ago when I was outside with Stephan and we were… well you know."

"Yes, let's not go into detail Amanda, he makes me feel sick. You'll bloody catch something one day."

"Shut your mouth you stupid bitch and listen to me for once will you!" Amanda shouted at the top of her voice. The cabbie's eyes matched hers in the rear-view mirror, and Kate immediately apologised for her friend's behaviour.

"Sorry mate, she's a bit pissed. I promise it won't happen again." After slowing the car down for a moment, the cabbie just shook his head in resignation and continued to drive.

"Well Kate, Stephan said that when he was in the gent's up on the Downs today, he heard some bloke in the cubicle telling someone on the phone to take a photograph of a safe in somebody's house. He said he even heard him explaining how you turn the power off at the mains."

"Stephan thought it sounded like this bloke was planning a robbery or something. He overheard everything. Anyway, this bloke eventually came out of the cubicle and Stephan, naturally assuming he might be a burglar or something, offered him a fix." Amanda screeched out a loud cackling laugh and pinched her nose before continuing.

"Yeah, come on, hurry up", Kate demanded utterly frustrated by her friend's long drawn out story, especially since it involved Stephan. "We're nearly home. Come on, get on with it," Kate pleaded as the driver turned the corner onto

Cleeve Hill, stopping a few yards from the house where she lived with her mother and stepfather.

"Well, as it turns out, that this bloke was a copper Kate, a Detective in the CID. He roughed Stephan up a bit for offering him drugs, shoved a warrant card in his face and then just let him go! He didn't nick him or anything. Now, take a wild guess what this copper's name was Amanda? Go on."

Kate was shaking from head to foot as the cold wind blasting down the hill gripped her. "Go on, hurry up, tell me," she said, holding the door open and looking up and down the dark road. "The driver's waiting."

"Andy, Kate, that's what his name was. Andy bloody McDermott. Your fucking dad!"

"My dad?" Kate asked, wide-eyed, poking a finger into her chest.

"Right first time Kate, your dad!" Amanda cackled as the taxi pulled away and drove up the hill.

17. Christi

Now, Christi Blake wasn't what one might describe as an ordinary copper. No, Christi was much more than that. Two unpublished books lay gathering dust in her dining room, penned between her time spent nappy changing, carrying out early morning feeds or cooking for her husband, Mike, and their twin girls. There's so much more to Christi Blake than just being just a plain old copper.

But far more important, Christi Blake has an excellent nose for sniffing out bent copper's, to the point where her colleagues covertly nicknamed her "Sniffer Blake", mainly the bent coppers that is.

Christi was a member of the *IAD*, the South West's *Internal Affairs Department*, and had recently attained the temporary rank of Detective Inspector. The promotion was to be confirmed upon her return from maternity leave following the birth of her twin girls, Ivy and Pearl. And today was that day for Christi, but it had come around far too soon for her liking. Mike and the two little angels were her life and secretly she wondered if she was doing the right thing.

Christi kissed both their matching foreheads, shedding a tear as her mother Margaret helped the girls wave their tiny little hands from the open porch of her parent's home in Filton, Bristol. Christi had flatly refused to return to shift work again, to the point where she'd threatened to resign from the force rather than do that again. Her thoughts were that *she'd brought them into the world and whatever happens they will always come first.*

So, for the first time in what had been a long and at times rewarding career she was going to be a nine-to-five copper. No more overtime, no more nights away sleeping on a *Lenny Henry* mattress in a soulless hotel room watching *Coronation Street.* No, from now on it was going to be either nine-to-five, or they could shove their promotion where the sun doesn't shine.

As usual, her husband Mike had been fully supportive, both of them sitting down one night over a couple of glasses of wine agreeing that if they were perfectly honest with each another, they didn't need the overtime, and with her recent promotion to Detective Inspector, they'd probably be better off. So, for Christi, back to the force it was. She was going back to head up the Internal Investigations Branch – she'd been offered the new role as a sort of *sweetener*. Good officer's like Christi Blake were extremely hard to come by.

Christi was used to being regarded with disdain and suspicion by her work colleagues. She'd become hardened, almost accustomed, to being shunned at the Christmas parties. That was, of course, if she was lucky enough to be invited in the first place.

So, her social life in the force was a lonely, solitary affair, and pretty much non-existent. But over the years she had become used to it and, put simply, she really didn't care anymore what her colleagues thought. They could all *jog on* in her book. Some poor sod had to sniff out the bent coppers because in her opinion there was nothing worse than a crooked cop. So, Sniffer Blake would carry on sniffing, regardless.

Turning the corner of Citrus Avenue, parking her new white Fiat 500C behind Redland police station, Christi was making her first official port of call in over eighteen months. A meeting had been arranged with her immediate boss. Her guvnor, Detective Chief Inspector Karen Cook.

As she entered the small reception area, the overweight uniformed Duty Sergeant standing behind the desk immediately recognised her and slammed his big leather-bound daybook shut with a loud *bang* as she approached.

"And for what do we owe this unexpected bloody pleasure Detective Sergeant Blake!" was his sarcastic greeting. "Long-time no see. Can't say we missed you." But the tall Sergeant didn't laugh, because he wasn't joking.

At five feet five and weighing less than nine stone wet, Christi Blake was the type of person you just didn't see coming. In a word, she was utterly fearless. Her well known temper and lightning wit preceded her everywhere she went. So, woe betide the copper that got in her way or purposely upset her. And this long-forgotten fat ranting moron just had.

She slammed her eyes at the Sergeant, remembering him for what he was before she'd left to go on maternity leave – an overweight, sexist pig!

"Firstly, Sergeant Tanner," she said, "if memory serves me right, the correct procedure would be to ask me for my warrant card. Wouldn't you agree Sergeant?"

The shaken Sergeant immediately pulled his shoulders back and stood rigid at attention nodding, as his mouth opened but nothing came out. His face turning a reddish hue. But Christi being Christi was far from finished. "So, in future Sergeant Tanner you will either address me as DI… Detective Inspector, or Ma'am, whichever you prefer. But never Sergeant, or any other title you can think of in that tiny little mind of yours. Now do I make myself clear Sergeant Tanner!"

"Yes, quite clear Ma'am, sorry I didn't realise you'd been promoted. I'm about to change shifts, been a long night Ma'am you understand," Sergeant Tanner felt hot. He looked hot.

"Good, so now we've got that little misunderstanding out of the way, this is my ID Sergeant," said Christi, holding her warrant card up close to his red, sweaty face. "And now I would like you to call up to Detective Chief Inspector Karen Cook and inform her that I'm here to see her. Do you think you can do that for me Sergeant?"

"Of course, Ma'am, sorry, I'll call and let her know straight away," the Sergeant replied, picking up the green internal telephone on his desk and not daring to utter another word. He was retiring in three months and he'd be doubly sure to keep well away from Christi Blake's path in the short time he had left.

As she entered the office, Karen's greeting was like that of a long-lost sister. She'd always been the one ally that Christi could rely on and had, for the most part, been responsible for Christi's recent promotion to Inspector. Although, like all new promotions in the force, it was *probationary*, subject to approval by the Chief Constable. Karen would pull out all the stops to ensure it went through smoothly.

"Really glad to have you back Christi, take a seat", Karen said, sitting down opposite her. "Now tell me all about the girls," she said, gleefully clapping her hands as Christi pulled her skirt taught and sat down.

"Must admit I'm glad to be back guv," Christi said, lying through her teeth. "And thanks for your support with my promotion, I really appreciate that."

"Not a problem Christi, you deserve it. You know we really missed you around here. But enough of that for now, how are the twins getting on?" Karen asked as her face lit up imagining their identical faces. She'd seen their pictures on Christi's Facebook page, but respectfully kept her distance, not wishing to burden her with any of the current cases while she was off enjoying maternity leave.

Christi had deserved her well-earned break following her last case, the arrest and successful conviction of two bent coppers convicted of taking bribes and holding back vital evidence against a well-known gangster, come drug pusher, in Taunton.

"The girls are just beautiful guv, they're two sweet little angels. But I'm sure all new mums say that," Christi said, sighing contently.

"You've called them Ivy and Pearl, haven't you? Oh, what lovely names, is Mike okay? Bet he loves being a dad if I know your Mike."

"Yeah, he's loving it, I just want him to bugger off and do some work. I think mum's loving it more though. She's looking after them today while I'm at work. Dad doesn't say a lot, but you know my dad, he never does. I did catch him feeding them half a fresh cream bun each the other day." They both laughed at that.

Christi could sense her boss was already bored with the conversation and would prefer to return to the work in hand. The signs were all there. Her eyes were glancing around the desk, she was becoming fidgety and she was fiddling nervously with a green case file lying on the desk. Her smile was diminishing, and Christi's natural instinct told her that "The lovely baby moment was well and truly over."

"Anyway, guv so what's new?" she asked, rubbing her hands excitedly. "What new and thrilling cases have you got lined up for me? I'm bursting to get my teeth into something."

"Well, I'm glad to hear that Christi", answered Karen in a nonchalant tone. "But I'm not sure if this will lead to anything. You see DS Pete Goodfield popped his head around the door yesterday morning. Now we all know Pete's a goody bloody two shoes at times, but deep down he's a damn good copper. Anyway, he asked me to take a look at this," Karen said, holding up the green file she'd been fiddling with earlier. "So, I did."

"Go on," replied Christi, her natural curiosity clearly aroused.

"Well it involves a Detective Sergeant Andy McDermott. You probably remember him from way back."

Christie did and sighed rolling her eyes. She could remember him all right from two years ago when he'd tried to

189

get into her knickers at Sergeant "Jock" McGuire's leaving do. She could also remember him constantly visiting the gent's and at the time suspected he was snorting cocaine or something. But it was Jock's retirement party so, for the good of all concerned, she decided to keep her mouth shut.

Karen continued, "It all started when a complaint was made about a Miss Rebecca Thorneycroft. The complaint was lodged with DS Mandy Smith who was on duty that day and took down her statement. She passed the complaint up the line to Peter who, in turn, asked Andy McDermott to take a look at it."

"Sorry guv, I'm a bit lost here, who made the complaint?" Christi tentatively asked.

"Well the complaint was made by a Mrs Elizabeth Baker whose mother had employed this Thorneycroft woman as her carer… companion… or whatever you want to call it. When her mother passed away, she left just over a hundred and seventy-five grand to Thorneycroft and she'd only been her carer for a couple of years. So, Mrs Baker found the whole thing a bit odd. She said, and I quote, 'my mother just wasn't the type of person to hand over money willy-nilly to an absolute stranger'."

Christi thought for a moment, fiddling with the hem of her skirt, before replying. "You said this Baker woman thought it was odd. Well I don't think it's odd guv. Sounds to me like sour grapes. Plain old-fashioned jealousy or something."

"Well that's exactly what Pete Goodfield thought at the time, so he passed it straight over to McDermott who, after interviewing Thorneycroft in Bath, came back with the same conclusion. So, all good… or so you'd think, yeah? Case closed… at least one would assume."

"Yeah," Christi replied, itching for her second cigarette in two years as she sat, still nervously playing with the hem of her knee-length skirt.

"Anyway," said Karen, "After McDermott finished interviewing Thorneycroft, so say off the record, he filed his report in the normal manner and recommended that no further action be taken. So, on paper, that all looks good."

"But…" Christi said, attempting to butt in and still confused.

"Hang on Christi, there's more," Karen said, holding up her hand. Christi continued to listen while but wondering if her painted red nails met regulations.

"Now this is where it all starts to get really bloody interesting Christi, because when Pete Goodfield closed the case file, he asked McDermott to instruct Valerie in records to file it away. You know, just in case something reared its head later on."

Christi pictured the Redland police station's confusing filing system in her mind.

"Yes, got that, go on guv."

"But you see he didn't Christi. Instead, he instructed Valerie to shred it! Luckily for us, and surprisingly enough, our system here does actually work. McDermott must have forgotten that old case files can't be shredded without either Pete Goldfield's signature or mine. So, without a signature and strictly following protocol, good old Veronica in records simply put it back on Pete's pile with a post-it it note stuck to the top."

"So, tell me Christi, why would McDermott do that? Why would he deliberately disobey a direct order from his DS?"

"I really don't know guv, could it have been a mistake? Maybe he heard him wrong, these things do happen."

"Granted, and at first that's exactly what I thought Christi, that was until our police divers found the body of Tom Thorneycroft, Rebecca Thorneycroft's stepfather, face down in the River Avon a week ago. And, when his flat was searched, over ninety thousand pounds in cash was found stashed under the carpet. Bit of a bloody coincidence that, don't you think?"

Christi sniffed…

18. McDermott

McDermott screwed his face up and perched his lips as the ice-filled gin and tonic invaded his taste buds. It was his fourth of the night.

"I can't believe you're driving home in that state, you wanker," said Rebecca, slamming her glass tumbler down onto the bar.

"Don't you go worrying about me Becks. Us coppers have what we call our own secret signal. We just flash our lights on and off a few times, then sit and watch as the blues and two's go flying by. Good eh?" McDermott made a *na-na* sound and laughed.

"Think I've heard that somewhere before, but it's the first time I've heard a copper be stupid enough to admit it. Even a pissed up one like you."

"Back to mine then Becks, is it?" McDermott asked, swallowing the last remnants of his drink.

"No, not tonight Andy! Tonight, is my night off, you're pissed, and I doubt very much if you'd be able to get it up! And if you really want to know, I'm getting fucking pissed off with…"

"Becks, Becks, aren't *we* forgetting something? You know, our little arrangement and all that?" Andy said, cutting her off and wagging his forefinger annoyingly close to her stolid looking face. She didn't flinch, but instead moved closer to him and, right at that moment, didn't give a hoot who heard her.

"No! And don't forget you're in this as deep as I am. It's me that's about to steal the best part of a hundred grand and give half to you. So, tonight Andy fucking McDermott you can go and do one! Dig the bitch up if you want. Go on dig her up! Because I really don't give a shit anymore! I've had enough! Oh, and while we're on the subject, and if you still want the money, our little arrangement's just come to an end. No more shagging me when you feel like it. No more! You got that!"

Rebecca slammed her glass down snarling as McDermott betrayed a look of total shock and resignation as he looked around the bar. He knew the day would come when the apprentice would turn on the sorcerer, but he didn't expect it to be today. Faking an unconvincing laugh, he quickly decided to try another tack.

"Okay, okay, calm down, don't get your knickers in a twist. Tell you what, let's change the subject shall we? How'd you fancy a bite to eat? We can sit down and chat things over while I take a look at the photos of the safe? I know just the place, it's only around the corner. Is Chinese okay?" he asked, playing on her penchant for Asian cuisine. Rebecca purposely delayed her response, enjoying this long overdue moment of clarity in their relationship.

"Just a chat and that's it," she firmly declared. "I'm deadly serious. No more blackmailing me. If I want to sleep with you, I will. If I don't, I won't. Now you got that?"

"Loud and clear Becks, loud and clear," he replied, thinking to himself, *there's still a glimmer of hope then.*

Uncle Wong's was one of the finer and more exclusive Chinese restaurants on Bristol's Park Street. Rebecca ordered her favourite shark fin soup followed by sweet and sour chicken and egg fried rice and looked on in disgust as McDermott gorged himself on a portion of barbecued spareribs, as thick brown sauce dripped from his chin.

Hoping he might take the hint by patting her mouth with a serviette, she picked up her iPhone and clicked the photo icon.

McDermott looked across. "Let's have a look then," he said, snatching it from her grasp and wiping his mouth. "Bloody amazing these things, aren't they?" he said. "Clear as a whistle, the clarity's amazing. Right, it looks like the safe's an El Diablo."

"It says that on the front dickhead," replied Rebecca, raising her eyebrows as she munched on a prawn cracker.

But McDermott had either chosen to ignore her comment or simply hadn't heard it as he continued to describe the safe. "Probably what… twenty years old and it's analogue all right. You know, mechanical like I said. So, that's all good. I should have the master combination for you by this time tomorrow night. So, when are *we* going to do this?"

We? Rebecca thought, wanting to question that remark but deciding not to.

"This weekend, when they're both asleep," she replied, searching her clutch bag for a cigarette.

"Okay, but that still leaves *us* with a problem, doesn't it? How are *you* going to get to the main switch in the hall cupboard without the camera seeing you? You can't trip over the door frame again. Bet you haven't thought of that one, have you my lovely?"

Ooh, my lovely is it. Come to heel you rotten evil bastard, Rebecca thought, nodding at the door before offering her sarcastic reply.

"Actually… *my lovely!"* she said, pouting her cherry red lips… "I'll tell you outside. Quick fag?"

Beneath the smoking shelter, she lit McDermott a Gitane and passed him the cigarette containing traces of her cherry lipstick. The smell of the strong French tobacco wafted through the air, spiralling out through the open wooden structure. By now, McDermott was in detective mode and drew hard on the cigarette, as his eyes narrowed, and he looked across at her.

"Go on then," he said, "Clever clogs, explain how you're going to do it."

"Simple," replied Rebecca, confidently blowing smoke into the air.

McDermott felt confused. He hadn't met this Rebecca before, and it worried him. It was almost like she didn't care what happened to her anymore. His instincts served him right because she didn't, because the worm had turned.

"Simple? McDermott asked, raising his eyebrows, "What do you mean simple? Believe me, the last thing I want is you to get caught. You see I think I'm falling for you…"

By now, Rebecca didn't give a hoot what he thought, or how he felt about her. So, cutting him off mid-sentence, she held up her hand placing him squarely on the back foot.

"Well, believe or not, it was Tom Thorneycroft who gave me the idea in the first place. I'm the first to admit that he wasn't what you might call the most honest or reliable of people, no. But he did know a thing or two about safes. When I was drying my hair in my room the other night, I remembered something he'd told me when I was a little girl. He'd come home pissed up one night and started rattling on about a time when he'd robbed a safe from a business unit, he was working in. He said he got away with ten grand, or at least that's what he told me."

"Anyway, the same as Enid's house this business unit was monitored by a CCTV system and didn't have a burglar alarm fitted, so he went back one night and blew the mains up by squirting water into an outside socket."

"He said there was an enormous flash and the whole place just died. You see, he'd blown the main circuit breaker inside by creating a short circuit from outside."

McDermott pulled hard on the remnants of his cigarette. Rebecca could sense his tortured brain whirling like a child's top as he analysed everything, searching for a reason to tell her the plan was a non-starter. She stood back and left him to his thoughts for a moment before explaining the next part of her plan.

"Now Archie said the wiring in Lonsdale is really old and needs replacing and even the slightest thing could trip that main switch. So why don't I just squirt water into the socket next to my bed and, *bang*, everything goes out. You know – the lights, the power, the cameras, everything!"

McDermott let out a low whistle. "I have to give it to you Becks, you really have thought this through, haven't you? I mean, I can't help you on this one, they won't give me the case. Bath isn't on my patch?" he said, happy that once more he'd found a clever way of distancing himself from the sharp end of the stick.

Convenient that, she thought, but she didn't really care who the hell investigated it. She could handle it on her own. She only really needed him for the combination so, stubbing out her cigarette in the ashtray on the wooden bench, she looked up and simply said, "So, the plans a goer then."

She'd heard his earlier declaration of love about "falling for her" all right, but that was just beer talk and it meant nothing to her. He'd raped her, blackmailed her, and treated her like a filthy whore since the first day they'd met. And the day was fast approaching when this fucker right in front of her, who was now acting like a lovesick puppy, would pay. She was in charge now. After all, what she knew about him could destroy his career overnight.

Deep down McDermott was a weak man, a pawn in a larger game she was playing. Rebecca intended to use that weakness and his pathetic declaration of undying love against him.

Come to me heel you bastard, she thought as he swamped her hands and stared into her eyes.

You idiot! As if I'm going to be Oliver bloody Twist again. What am I now… Bonnie bloody Parker?

Snatching her hands away, she looked him straight in the eye. "That was my last drink tonight," she said, faking a yawn and stretching her arms. "So, I'm off home now. You can get the bill. Think I'll have an early night."

Clyde wasn't smiling this time…

19. Kate

McDermott turned the corner onto Cleeve Hill and parked up outside number forty. The grand white facade with its thirties style rounded corners and "Art deco" Crittal windows stared back at him through the leafiness of the weeping willow trees on the drive. The same drive where he used to clean his car when Kate was a little girl.

He looked through the windscreen and watched as the front door opened and Kate emerged wearing a long floral skirt and a short black leather jacket, the one he'd bought her for her eighteenth birthday. Her head was down, and her usual wave and welcoming smile were strangely absent.

He could see Kate's mother hiding behind the curtains, watching from the darkness of the lounge. They hadn't spoken a word since their messy divorce, following his ex-wife's conversation with one of her so-called *friends,* who'd been more than happy to furnish her with all the sordid details concerning his numerous affairs and cocaine abuse. He could see her dark outline behind the curtains, watching, protecting her daughter as she always had.

As she approached, McDermott reached across, pulled the door handle on his tattered old Audi convertible and Kate climbed in, offering a last lingering wave towards the moving curtains.

"Hiya love, give us a kiss then, really missed you I have?"

But Kate didn't answer and didn't even look at him. Instead, she continued to glare out of the passenger window and a few seconds later ordered him to, "Drive will you, we need to talk."

Raising his eyebrows and without offering a response, he engaged drive and started to move off up the hill. The silence was deafening, hanging like a cloud in the tiny car and, after travelling less than a few yards, he snapped, "All right then, c'mon tell me what's happened this time, boyfriend trouble again is it?"

"No, this time it's not! This time it happens to be more about you than about me dad!" she declared, folding her arms and slamming her eyes.

"Okay, so what's your mother been saying about me now?" he demanded, punching the steering wheel and causing her to recoil in her seat. He accelerated faster up the hill. Crossing the lights at the top, they pulled into the Bull and Bear pub where earlier he'd booked a table for two as part of a birthday surprise, he was planning for her, and afterwards was going to be shopping at the Mall in Cribbs Causeway. Kate, like her mother, was addicted to shopping.

Parking in the far corner of the busy car park and turning the ignition off, McDermott made an awkward attempt at putting his arm around her. But his fatherly approach was firmly rebuked as she pushed him away and leant her head against the side passenger window, her eyes now streaming with tears.

So, he asked her again, "What's going on Kate? Come on tell me, for Christ's sake! What have I done this time!"

Her whole body was physically shaking as she looked across at him, the corners of her mouth curling downwards. As she mumbled her words, a line of spittle dropped to the seat from her lips.

"What the hell are you up to this time dad?" she demanded. "What are you involved with now? Are things that bad you need to rob someone? Tell me, are they? Answer me!" she screamed in disgust.

"What the hell are you going on about Kate… robbing someone?" said McDermott, his detective mind already starting to work overtime as he tried to figure out how she knew. More importantly, who had told her. Then suddenly like a flash it came to him and he remembered the hoody. *It has to be him; he must have heard me on the phone after all. He's about the same age as Kate. Shit, she probably knows him.*

McDermott didn't say anything for a moment and just stared through the windscreen at the swaying pub sign rocking from side to side in the breeze. It wasn't the first time he'd been caught out like this. His ex-wife, Penny, was a past master at it.

"Come on Kate, spill the beans, tell me what you're going on about so we can both get some lunch," he asked, lowering his voice to a smoother and more acceptable tone, an old interviewing technique of his which seemed to work as Kate shifted her body towards his at the same time as drying her eyes with his hankie.

"Well, when I was at *La Toya* the other night this scumbag drug dealer, Stephan Earl, from St Augustine's took my friend outside for… well drugs, amongst other things, and told my friend, Amanda, that he'd heard you in the toilet on the Downs spouting off to someone about robbing a house. She said you

206

were giving instructions on how to photograph a safe. This, Stephan said, it was definitely you because you beat him up a bit and shoved your warrant card in his face. So, tell me dad, are you going to rob someone?"

McDermott let out a fake laugh, still stalling for time as he stared out through the misted-up windscreen.

"You are joking, aren't you?" was all he could think of to say. But Kate was having none of it.

"Are you planning a robbery? Answer me! Are you?" she screamed, banging her small hand down on the dash.

"Look, love, I didn't want you to worry about me, but it's my job," he said, letting out a gentle sigh. "Sometimes I have to go undercover and, yes, Stephan was telling you the truth, it was me on the phone in the toilet. It's part of an investigation I'm working on. I shouldn't even be telling you this. If my guvnor found out, he'd have my balls for book ends."

"So, there's nothing going on then dad?" Kate asked, still sniffing in a slightly calmer tone. "Is that what you're saying? I've been out of my mind with worry and I couldn't talk to anyone. Amanda's such a bitch. She actually enjoyed telling me. What a cow! I'm so sorry dad, I really am."

Kate reached over and McDermott gently kissed her on the forehead. They sat in silence for a moment, him deep in thought as he stroked Kate's hair planning on how he'd rid himself of that drug dealing bastard, Stephan Earl.

He wouldn't lay a finger on her friend, Amanda. That would be too obvious. According to Kate, she was just a dirty old scumbag druggie who'd probably be dead soon anyway. And who'd believe her word against his? No, it was Stephan that needed sorting. And it had to be quick.

"So, you haven't mentioned this to anyone then love?" he asked. "Not even your mother? I mean, if this got out it would fold the case and could ruin my career," he added, still gently stroking her hair.

"No dad, no one, I swear to you. I hate Amanda and that fucking Stephan; he's going to end up in the gutter that bastard."

"Stop swearing love," he said. *You're right, but it's going to be a very deep one… the River Avon.*"

20. Binnie

Now Binnie Walters took care of things. Things that the so-called *ordinary* people in society simply couldn't or simply wouldn't. He was nicknamed *Binnie* the night of his seventeenth birthday, after depositing a lifeless body into an empty *wheelie bin* on Bristol's lively Gloucester Road.

Apparently, or as the story went at the time, a doorman had made the mistake of refusing him entry to a nightclub. So, Binnie waited patiently around the corner, hiding in a dark alley for over two hours. Then he attacked the twenty stone doorman from behind using a house brick as he made his way home.

Even back then, Binnie wasn't what one could describe as small, not by any means. Standing at six feet two, weighing in at just under seventeen and a half stone and with bright ginger hair, Binnie stood out. He was more than a handful for anyone.

The very next morning, a council worker had discovered the blood-soaked body upside down in a wheelie bin, and it wasn't long before the police were knocking on his mother's front door in Keynsham, Bristol.

From then on, the nickname had *Binnie* stuck, and the legend was born. But that was way back then. Binnie had changed, moved on so to speak. Nine gruelling years spent in the squalor of Horfield Prison's "D" Wing paid testament to that. Binnie was careful now. Wheelie bins leave fingerprints, but more importantly than that they left his DNA.

Binnie's real name was William Spencer Walters and only a few chosen individuals knew that. More importantly an old acquaintance of his, Detective Sergeant Andy McDermott of Redland CID, knew that.

Binnie took care of McDermott's mess and made things go away, disappear so to speak. In return, and within reason, McDermott turned a blind eye and allowed him a free reign to trade his drugs and protection rackets in the back streets and seedy nightclubs of Bristol's underworld. All for a cut of course. McDermott had set up the meeting with Binnie at a deserted spot underneath a disused concrete water tower on the Bristol Downs, not far from the toilets where he'd encountered Stephan Earl a few weeks before.

A thirty mile an hour gale was whistling through the trees and the birds were strangely absent as he stood alone staring out into the darkness underneath the monolithic grey structure.

The meeting had been arranged for the stroke of midnight, and the illuminous dials on his Seiko watch confirmed that Binnie was already five minutes late. McDermott shivered in the cold, pulling his collar up taught around his neck as he shouted into the darkness.

"Binnie, you there mate? It's me Mac. If you're there, say something." McDermott's voice echoed around the concrete structure; his hands trembled as he felt for the protection of the thousand-volt Taser in his pocket. "Binnie!!" he shouted, once again checking his watch.

"I'm right behind you Mac," boomed a loud gruff voice that he instantly recognised as Binnie's. Only Binnie called him Mac.

McDermott nearly jumped out of his skin and turned around to find he was staring straight into the cold blue eyes of the one and only Binnie Walters. He'd been only a foot away the whole time, hiding behind a concrete leg of the tower. Binnie had enjoyed listening to McDermott's laboured breathing, harvesting the sounds of fear and thought it was funny that he was shaking like a leaf from head to foot and nearly dancing on the spot.

"Fuck me Binnie!" McDermott blew out "I nearly had a fucking heart attack man. How long you been there?"

"Long enough to know that you're shitting yourself Mac. I could almost smell it running down your leg," Binnie said, letting out a deep growling laugh as he placed his huge paw on Andy's shoulder, pulling him in towards him, shaking hands. Binnie's grip was titanic, a firm, no-nonsense handshake and McDermott prayed to God he'd never be added to Binnie's so-called *hit list*.

"So, what seems to be the problem this time Mac? You sounded right panicky on the phone earlier," he asked as McDermott lit a cigarette. The acrid smell reminded Binnie of the *Two's landing* in Horfield prison, his accommodation provided free of charge by the Home Office to the lifers, and the most hardened of the City's convicted murderers, rapists, and drug dealers. Sensing Binnie's angst and taking one last lingering draw, McDermott threw it down onto the wet grass, screwed it into the mud and moved a foot back apologising.

"Sorry Binnie, forgot you hate cigarettes."

"Mac, enough of the polite bullshit, it doesn't suit you. So, come on, tell me what's up this time? The boys told me the last old git you sent our way put up one a hell of a fight. They had to hold his head under the water for a good five minutes before he croaked it. So, come on, tell me who's for the chop this time ah?"

"Stephan Earl, that's who," McDermott curtly replied.

Binnie whistled loudly; the high-pitched sound lost to the screeching wind still rushing through the tower.

"Stephan Earl? Are you fucking kidding!" Binnie snapped. "His family are like the fucking Mafia round here. If one of his brothers found out I'd topped him, I'd be dead in a New York minute."

The Earls were legends in their own right. There'd been an undeclared truce between Binnie's boys and the Earls on the streets of Bristol for years. They were careful to stay their side of the street, as long as Binnie and his mob stayed on theirs. Knowing it was a really big ask and he was skating on thin ice, McDermott decided to try another approach.

"You're starting to scare me now Binnie? I mean, I can always ask someone else to do my tidying up, you know, and we can just forget all about our little arrangement."

Although utterly terrified of Binnie, McDermott was probing, taunting him. But Binnie was far from fazed.

"Don't you fucking threaten me!" he said, growling and moving himself closer to McDermott. "We might have a little arrangement but just you remember it's only me and you out here tonight, and don't think for one tiny minute that fucking Taser in your pocket will save you."

McDermott tightened his grip on the Taser and retreated a step back.

"Binnie, Binnie," McDermott pleaded, holding out his hands. "Look, unless Stephan Earl goes away and quick, I'm going to end up in the big house myself, and that ain't good for either of us, now is it? I mean, I can't protect you from the inside of a prison cell, can I?"

Binnie, deep in thought, looked McDermott straight in the eye, pulling on his chin like he always did when he felt cornered. He wanted a favour in return. This was a big ask and he'd have to take care of it himself. Even the likes of *Big Roy*, his right-hand man, couldn't know anything about this. So, he stood for a moment scheming, revelling as he always did in the unfolding drama.

"Well Mac, I'll have to take care of this one myself. Nobody, and I mean nobody, can know about it or we'll both for the knacker's yard. So, it's going to cost you, I want uh…"

Binnie looked up at the grey circling clouds. "First, I want ten grand in cash, then those trumped up charges against my brother dropped. That's the deal Mac, and that's the only way this is going to happen."

McDermott had known Binnie for years and recognised the greediness of his demands, knowing full well that money was the real issue here. Binnie was nobody's fool and was bright enough to realise that getting a manslaughter charge dropped against his brother, after he'd knocked down and killed two eighty-year-old pedestrians while four times over the limit, was nigh on impossible.

So, McDermott rightly interpreted the "get my brother released" part as a ploy and more of a gentle squeeze to lever even more money out of him.

"I can agree to the money Binnie, but we both know there's nothing I can do about Mark's manslaughter charges. That's way above my pay grade. Your brother's going up the big house for a long time and they wouldn't give a toss if I was the Chief Constable. They're going to throw the book at him."

McDermott waited for Binnie's reply, rightly sensing what was coming next. Just as he thought, and right on cue, Binnie raised his price.

"If that's the case, the price just went up to fifteen grand, and not a penny less." Binnie didn't say another word, just stood there staring menacingly at him. The money excited him, but it was more the game that he relished. But, very cleverly, McDermott had left the best for last.

"Okay Binnie, I can agree to the extra money but, before we shake hands, there's one more thing we need to agree on."

"There always is with you Mac. Go on get on with it."

"His body needs to disappear. *We* can't leave any traces. It has to look like he just got up one morning and decided to piss off to somewhere like America or something. There can't be any loose ends."

Binnie laughed at McDermott's last statement, rightly interpreting it as inferring a joint involvement. He simply replied, "it's not *we* Mac though, is it? It's just *me*."

Clearly, Binnie realised this meant either an acid bath or his body with a pair of concrete boots attached dumped far out at sea. So, for a moment he contemplated raising the price again. But he wasn't stupid and knew McDermott held some pretty good cards of his own. Hiring boats was expensive, traceable and incredibly risky, so it would have to be an acid bath. Stephan Elias Earl would simply disappear off the face of the earth. Without trace. And that would be that.

"Okay, but just remember one thing, it's only you and me that know anything about this. If it gets out and the Earl's come knocking on my door, I'll make fucking sure you're the next on their list. You got that Mac?"

Swallowing hard, McDermott pictured himself being macheted to death on a dark street, late at night.

Binnie could see the fear slowly etching across McDermott's face.

"Okay Binnie, I got that, so the deal's done then, yeah? You'll have the cash by this time tomorrow night. I'll call you when I've got it. When's this going to happen? The sooner the better for me."

"Two days Mac, give me two days, but then no more for a while ah. You're beginning to be regular. I'll have to start offering you discounts at this rate."

Binnie roared with laughter, but McDermott shivered as both men shook hands and walked off in opposite directions. The deal was done, and Stephan Earl was now officially amongst the walking dead…

21. Rebecca

It had to be tonight. Archie played darts for the *Greyhound* on Saturday nights and, like something out of the movie *Groundhog Day*, at eight o'clock on the dot, regular as clockwork, he'd shout *bye* to Enid at the top of his voice and, just after eleven, he'd stagger back through the front door three sheets to the wind. Simple as that.

Then, systematically he'd check the downstairs windows were locked and make sure the red video player light was on before finally, and what seemed like the umpteenth time, he'd rattle the front door and check the latch was across. Then, and only then, did he wander slowly off to bed. You could set your watch by him; the man was a human metronome.

McDermott had given Rebecca the six-digit emergency combination to the safe, telling her that under no circumstances was she to write it down. She'd memorised it *eight-six-one-nine-five-eight.*

It was now quarter past eleven and Archie's uneven footfalls echoed up the stairs. He was whistling to himself and obviously drunk. *Give it ten minutes, he'll be tucked up fast asleep and the snoring will start.*

Archie slammed the bedroom door, shaking the house to its foundations, then he started coughing and shuffling around before the all too familiar sound of his size tens hit the floor with a *crump, crump*. Finally, a noise sounding more like an African water buffalo than a yawn resonated through the dividing wall.

Ten minutes later the noise was replaced with an inert bothering stillness, coupled with a numbing silence filling the room. But it didn't last long, because after that came the snoring.

In an out, in an out. Waaahh! ... Waaahh! ...

At this time on any other Saturday night, she would be safely tucked up in bed with her earphones plugged in listening to music. Tonight, was very different, however, because tonight her life was going to change inexorably, and things would never be the same again.

She sat up and leant across the bed, switched on her bedside light and removed the Marigold gloves from the drawer she'd taken from the kitchen earlier. She then wrapped the dressing gown around her nakedness and shivered in the chilliness of the room. She remembered the carrier bag she'd need for later, so she reached down and pulled it out from under the bed and placed it in her dressing gown pocket. She looked across at the old Bakelite socket at the far side of the bed. The switch was already down, so all she needed to do was spray the water and, *bang*, she'd be off.

Only silence remained, occasionally disturbed by the rhythmical sounds of Archie's incessant snoring as the noise travelled through the wall. *Waaahh! ... Waaahh! ...*

Rebecca picked up the water bottle and, in one controlled movement, pressed the trigger and *crack!* a bluish-grey puff of smoke was spiralling through the air as the socket sparked and sizzled, releasing a greyish puff of smoke as the bed side lamp flashed once and went out.

Walking over to the window in the darkness, she pushed the sash gently upwards and instantly the freezing night air rushed in, lifting the front of her dressing gown as her naked body shivered. The branches of the willow trees were swaying back and forth, whistling in the night's breeze. Everything was silent, lifeless, as she stared out onto the deserted lawn. *Just me*, she thought.

Turning around and stopping mid-way between the window and the door, Rebecca placed her ear to the dividing wall and could hear Archie grunting, moaning and snoring in his bed. He was fast asleep. Reaching the bedroom door, she turned the brass knob slowly clockwise, pulling it towards her as the hinges released a low-pitched moan threatening the deafening silence. She glanced at the camera at the top of the landing. The red light was off. Only her and the darkness remained. She felt invisible.

Just me, she thought.

Feeling for the round wooden newel on the top of the stairs, she started the descent to the bottom hallway, careful to miss out the fifth tread, the one that had earlier announced Archie's drunken arrival. The stairs seemed to go on forever, the yellowing glare from the streetlights outside shining through the opaque glass door, lighting up the treads as she crept further down.

She could feel an unwanted agitation enter her body. Raw fear was trying to consume her being, when suddenly from above she could hear Archie coughing. She instantly froze as everything stopped and she stood rigid, utterly terrified. For a minute that felt more like five, she was rooted to the spot, too scared to turn around and too terrified to carry on. She prayed Archie wasn't behind her. *Don't be behind me! Please… How do I explain this?* She could almost picture him shouting at her. *"So, what do you think you're doing down there creeping around the house at this time of night Rebecca? Answer me! Enid! Enid, call the police."* *Sleep walking?* she wondered. Still only the silence remained. *Just me.*

From deep down inside, she mustered up enough courage to carry her to the bottom of the stairs as her bare feet sank to the depths of the thick Axminster carpet underfoot. She turned the handle to the lounge and it slowly opened.

Opening the door enough to squeeze through her small frame, she crept the last thirty feet or so towards the back of the room, towards the bookshelf and the money. The room had an almost supernatural glare to it. The streetlights outside were shining through the red velvet curtains, colouring it a deep reddish hue, likening the room to a scene from an old horror movie.

As she reached the bookcase, she quickly glanced behind her checking she was still alone before turning and running her thin spindly fingers along the third shelf up. She stopped as she reached *War and Peace* and wiggled it. The books were tightly packed. She had to tug at them to prize them free. Suddenly, they fell to the thick carpet below with a dull echoey *thud*. Once more she froze, listening, looking up at the ceiling waiting for sounds. But still there was nothing.

Just me.

The shiny aluminium safe at the back of the tunnel with its cylindrical dial stared invitingly back at her. It felt as though it was beckoning her to reveal what was inside. The room was bitterly cold, and she could see her breath dancing in the yellowing light. She reached in and surrounded the big silver dial with her gloved hand, then turned the dial clockwise and listened for the ominous *click*! as it reached the number eight, all the while McDermott's voice saying. *"Now turn it anti-clockwise to the six, Rebecca."* Click. *"Now turn it clockwise till you hear another."* Click. *Now turn it anti-clockwise again."* Click. *Then once more anti-clockwise."* Click. *Now the final one, the eight."* Click.

The safe omitted a dull *whirring* noise that sounded like an old clock unwinding itself and the door suddenly swung open with a mechanical *clunk*.

Don't stop now, open it up, open it…

Sweat beads ran down her forehead. She wiped her hands on her housecoat and she felt clammy. Her armpits were sopping wet, but the room was freezing. She gripped hold of the cold steel handle, pulled it towards her and probed the insides with her fingertips. And then she saw it… stack upon stack of money was piled high inside!

There must be thousands in there! she thought, trying to contain her excitement and not dance on the spot. She stared at the wad upon wad of crispy fifty-pound notes, packed like sardines in a John West factory, filling the inside from top to bottom. Each one neatly wrapped up in its own *Coutts Bank* paper sleeve.

Enid, you little beauty!

Pulling out the scrunched-up carrier bag from the inside of her dressing gown counting as she went, she started to place them in the bag one by one.

Thirty, thirty-one, two, three, thirty-four! Thirty-four times five thousand, that's a… a hundred and seventy grand. I love you Enid. I'll tell McDermott it was a hundred grand. Bollocks to him!

As she reached in to check that she'd removed all the money, she felt something like a bag with a string attached at the back of the safe. She pulled it out. *It has to be the diamonds!* Her eyes lit up. *Diamonds!!*

Being extremely quiet and carefully closing the safe door, she spun the dial fully clockwise and the safe omitted a *clunking, whirring* noise as it locked itself.

She looked in the bag which was smaller than the palm of her hand. She could feel two objects inside. She turned it upside down and shook it as two thumb-size cylindrical objects bounced into her outstretched palm. They were diamonds all right, and were as cold and raw as they came, uncut in their basic form. She held them up to the yellow streetlights where the colours formed prisms that danced and bounced across the room.

"Shit you little beauties," she mumbled, admiring the two objects that represented such wealth, power and a wonderful future.

Placing them back in the bag, she pulled the drawstring tight and put the bag in her pocket. She carefully placed the books back in exactly the same position she'd found them. Then she crept across the dimly lit room towards the door.

Stealing a quick look up towards the landing to check the light on the hall camera was still out, she quietly, step by step, started climbing the stairs. *I'm so happy. I've never felt so happy. I'll tell McDermott there was eighty grand in there. He'll never know. And the diamonds are mine. My share's going straight into my little hideaway. Fuck you, McDermott… Told you I'd get you back.*

22. Stephan

St Augustine's was a popular haunt for people seeking a quick fix, casual sex or even a weapon. And woe betide the brave naïve stranger who walked the streets at night without back-up or protection. But the Earls didn't need to worry about any of that because for years now they'd ruled their patch with an iron fist, paid off anybody that was anybody, and could walk the streets at night peddling their wears without fear of incumbrance or arrest.

They'd spent an obscene amount of money building up such a fearsome reputation, the threat of death or a near-death experience was their body armour. Those who were brave enough, or even stupid enough, to not pay heed would simply disappear, lost in the crime-ridden fog that consumed St Augustine's.

The crumbling Victorian facades hid the true misery, the shabby drawn curtains, overgrown front gardens and smashed streetlights, a clue to the real story. St Augustine's was a place where folk simply existed. You couldn't have what one might call a normal family life. Certainly not one you'd brag about to your friends over a glass of wine.

In the last few years, the developers had moved in and several of the dated old buildings had been hastily converted into flats or divided up into cramped over-priced bedsits. The poor and the unemployed made up ninety per cent of the tenants which led to St Augustine's being awarded the unwanted accolade of having the highest recorded crime rate in the city.

Hard drug use was spiralling out of control and, as a direct result, the murder rate had trebled in two years. For the poor kids trying to survive this *Hell's kitchen of the South West* anything resembling a normal family life was a mere daydream. Thoughts of regular employment or a decent education had been substituted in their formative years for artistic talents such as graffiti or the ability to roll the perfect spliff. The destructive energy that surrounded St. Augustine's sucked the soul from anybody even remotely connected with its dangerous streets.

Closely impersonating a dark hooded assassin, Stephan Earl sold his tightly drawn wraps of white powder to the kids, tramps and the homeless. In fact, he'd happily sell it to anyone desperate for a fix. The drugs were packed into neatly folded, see-though pouches and in reality, were a cut down mix of talcum powder, detergent or whatever was close at hand.

Pure cocaine, or *Columbian marching powder* as his street vendors termed it, made up only a quarter of the toxic wrap.

Taking special care of the drugs and sex side of the family business was Stephan's responsibility and in fairness he was extremely good at it, a natural one might say. Stephan guarded his territory jealously. If sex was your preference, then that wasn't a problem either. Only recently he'd recruited Amanda to the fold and several of his so-called *regulars* were enjoying the new girl in town. Some as many times as eight or nine times a night. But Amanda didn't care. After all, she'd progressed, moved on so to speak, and taken that simple leap of faith from crack cocaine to heroin, or brown's, as it was called on the streets.

Amanda's body lay like a frozen china doll sprawled amongst the damp sheets in her squalid bedsit. Now and again she'd wake up sensing a movement as, yet another unknown stranger entered her thin soulless body. All that remained of her tortured mind were vague memories of a family she'd once known. All conscious thoughts were by now shamefully absent.

Terence was the eldest of the three brothers and he saw himself as the clever one, their sort of unelected leader. Consequently, Terry took special care of the protection side of the business. He and his *night ghouls* would happily pay you a visit, provide you with a verbal quotation and tell you how they were going to protect your club, restaurant or business. All for a fee of course. And the fee needed to be paid weekly in arrears and, if you refused to pay or simply couldn't, Terry would become extremely agitated and a few days later you'd be introduced to David...

David Earl was the enforcer and his favourite ploy was targeting your family. So, when you were home cooking, doing the ironing or cleaning the windows you'd look up at the clock and think *the kids are late home tonight.* And about an hour later they'd bounce into the kitchen scaring you half to death by telling mummy and daddy that "Two really nice men took us to the park after school today mummy, to feed the ducks. And the nice men said to tell mummy and daddy that the pond is very cold, very deep and we must be really careful not to fall in. But don't worry mummy they were really nice men."

So, nine times out of ten and usually the next day mummy and daddy would pay up. And so, it went on.

231

Tonight though, Stephan thought it would be nice to pay Amanda a little visit in her filthy basement room he'd so kindly rented for her at the end of Gulliver Street. As he arrived, he found the front door was slightly ajar and wondered if it may have been her last client.

Amanda was pretty much bed bound. Her naked body was sprawled across the filthy bed, the knotted sheets just covering her once womanly curves. A pungent smell of stale alcohol mixed with sex filled the air, dozens of used condoms lay scattered across the filthy carpet, her body curled into a foetal position. She was completely comatose.

Stephan looked down at the thin listless body. The sickening sight of her protruding collar bones stretching the skin across her tiny worn out frame made him feel nauseous. He pulled the sheet over her, not sure if he'd felt guilty or he' done it in preparation for her next client.

"Don't worry Mand, it won't be long now," he whispered, squeezing her thin breast and greedily stuffing the scrunched-up twenty's, tenner's and five-pound notes into his pocket from the drawer at the side of the bed.

Just recently Bill Blake, Amanda's distraught father, had been poking his nose around asking particularly awkward questions at a few of the local bars and clubs and he'd been paying particular attention to *La Toya*. Stephan was becoming nervous and he'd be sure to ask his brother, David, to pay him a visit and tell him to "Fuck off and forget all about her! That's if you want to see your family again." Nine times out of ten the threats worked, even when used against high profile, ex-Tory councillors.

Closing the basement door and climbing the stone steps into the night, Stephan zipped up his collar and took a quick glance up and down the deserted street before beginning his short walk to *La Toya*. Confidently striding up Gulliver Street and rounding the corner onto the busy Gloucester Road, Stephan failed to notice the pile of rags in the dimly lit shopfront that held out an empty cake tin with an outstretched palm.

Binnie Walters pulled himself up from the filth-ridden floor, held a can of *Special Brew* to his lips and took a huge mouthful, watching as his quarry ran up the steps and entered the *La Toya*. Binnie had all the patience in the world. He'd be sure to wait as long as it took and sat himself down on the rain-sodden wooden bench, once more merging into the dismal surroundings.

An hour later, faking a loud snoring noise, he was still watching as Stephan emerged from the club. Apart from a few people inside the Kentucky opposite and an empty taxi on the other side of the road, all Stephan saw was a filthy tramp on a bench opposite. So, as he started his brief walk back to his brand-new luxury apartment on the corner of Rodway Street, he didn't hear the tramp following from behind.

Not a bad day, he thought, *six up, so that makes three grand for the week. Bring on the weekend.*

Feeling for the keys in his pocket, and at the same time quickening his pace, Stephan turned the corner onto Rodway Street, and it was then that he heard the sound of heavy footfalls behind. So, he turned to face the noise and that's when he saw him, the tramp that is. Only this time the tramp was holding a baseball bat. He was swinging it wildly above his head and trying extremely hard to make contact with Stephan's head. Stephan ducked instinctively and slammed his body into the metal railings, narrowly avoiding the tramp's first attempt.

"God, shit! What the fuck?" he screamed, as the tramp lifted the bat a for second time and its hardwood shaft connected squarely with Stephan's forehead. Stephan's world suddenly turned an oily black as he collapsed onto the wet pavement.

Amanda's father, the indomitable Bill Blake, who'd been following Stephan since he'd left the club, was hiding across the street behind a telephone box and watched as Binnie lifted Stephan's body onto his shoulder and threw it into the back of the old transit like a side of ham. Bill was happy with that, *must have upset somebody pretty bad this time*, he thought, *last, we'll see of you, you evil bastard.* He called an ambulance for Amanda as the transit sped off.

Stephan came to and found he was tied to an old dentist chair in the centre of the concrete floor in Binnie's lock up. Instinctively, he tried to touch his forehead, but couldn't because tightly drawn cable ties were biting into his bare flesh and he could feel his blood dripping slowly to the dust covered floor.

"Where am I?" he grunted, his eyes gradually adjusting to the dim light provided by the single fluorescent tube dangling on chains above his blood-soaked head. His breathing was laboured and slow as the grimy lock-up gradually came into focus. He was just able to identify an outline of a figure standing close to him.

"It's me Stephan, Binnie Walters. You must remember me?" Stephan was utterly petrified. The shadows cast across the dimly lit room felt confusing as the blurred outline of Binnie's face gradually came into focus, the eerie light colouring his bright ginger hair a strange reddish hue.

During all the time they'd shared the St Augustine's streets, he'd always been careful to heed his brother's advice to keep well away from Binnie, even crossing the street if he approached. "Don't fuck about with Binnie Walters," he'd told him. "Keep out of his way and he'll keep out of yours." So, why but, more importantly, why now?

"What the fuck's going on Binnie?" Stephan pleaded. "I ain't got no got no bitch with you man… What's going down?"

"Stephan," Binnie calmly replied as he walked menacingly closer, "I ain't got no *bitch* with you either. I mean it ain't like I can't handle the competition is it? Well not from a bunch of amateurs like you lot. This is about money Stephan. Nothing else, just money. Believe me, none of this is personal because if it was, you'd be screaming your fuckin' head off by now. But it's not, so just sit back and try and relax."

"Relax? Are you fucking mad?" Stephan screamed at the top of his voice, writhing around in the chair. "Not personal! My brother's will fucking kill you! You're fucking mad…!"

Binnie laughed and cut him off with a wave of his finger only a foot from his tortured face and bulging eyes. "Don't call me mad Stephan! That's twice you've called me mad! Don't say it again or trust me this *will* get personal and I'll slice you up like a pig. This is going to be quick! I can promise you that, I've gone to an awful lot of trouble here. I've even prepared you a nice bath afterwards."

Binnie thought that was funny and laughed, the fluorescent light accentuating a yellowing of his normally pearly white teeth creating a ghoulish appearance adding to his abject terror. Frantic beyond words, hyperventilating, unadulterated fear suddenly gripped hold of Stephan as he struggled to free himself from the dentist chair. The round metal base was rocking noisily backwards and forwards on the concrete floor as he screamed out again, "In your dreams you bastard, you're dead! Dead! I'll fucking kill you!"

But Binnie didn't even wince. A few seconds later, Stephan's empty threats were replaced with heart-wrenching sobs as he began to plead for his life. "Binnie, please, pleeeeease mate! I'll do anything, anything! If it's money you want, I've got plenty! How much are they paying you? I'll double it, treble it even. Please, please don't do this mate!"

Binnie just tutted and shook his head, finding it amusing that this so-called terror of the streets from St Augustine's was now tied to an old dentist chair, begging for his life. Binnie noticed that Stephan's urine had stained his jeans and ran onto the concrete floor below. Binnie didn't like that. Oh no, Binnie detested uncleanliness in any form so, shaking an empty blue plastic container an inch from Stephan's face, he said "You dirty bastard, you're pissing all over my clean floor."

"And the answer's no, I can't take your money. In my book a deal is a deal, so sorry *mate* I can't really help you. I mean what would they say if I went around double crossing everyone. I'd be out of business in twenty-four hours. No, Stephan, first come first served, that's always been my motto."

"Anyway, let's get back to the business in hand. See this little sticker on the side of the container I'm holding?" Stephan nodded as his eyes fixed on the container. "Well this small

238

writing just below the skull and crossbones states quite clearly that, under European law, all hazardous liquids including sulphuric acids like these should be safely stored away in a sealed container like this one," he said menacingly, shaking the empty container an inch from Stephan's face.

"Oh, sorry Stephan, no need to worry, this one's empty. All the full ones are over there," informed a wide-eyed Binnie, pointing at ten plastic containers stacked high in the corner with foaming acid leaking onto the concrete floor.

Stephan looked across at the containers and let out a blood-curdling scream. "Help, help, heeeelp, help me someone! Oh God, no, no, help me someone!" He started to rock the chair's heavy metal base backwards and forwards until eventually he'd built enough momentum for it to topple backwards, his head smashing onto the concrete floor with a dull *thud*.

Stephan lay quite still and motionless. The only thing he could hear was a steady monotone note from his ears. All feelings of desperation seemed to have evaporated as pure hopelessness and a form of acceptance entered his thoughts as the grip of the ties cut even deeper into his flesh.

Binnie stared down at his unworthy prey, revelling, delighted by the sheer unadulterated terror that the awful moment had delivered. He watched as Stephan writhed around on the concrete floor and kicked out in one last feeble attempt at freedom. Binnie picked up the baseball bat and, without further utterance or warning, lifted the shiny hardwood shaft high above his head and brought it squarely down onto the centre of Stephan's head. The sheer momentum of the impact caused his skull to smash onto the concrete floor and produced a dull squelching sound not too dissimilar to an exploding melon as millions of tiny bone fragments entered his brain. Stephan's screaming pleas for his pitiful existence instantly ceased.

And the apparently immortal, almost God-like figure of Stephan Elias Earl, the youngest of the Earl family aged just twenty-two, lay dead, tied to an old dentist chair, his head smashed to a red watery pulp, his life expunged.

Binnie blew out and pulled a starched white handkerchief out of his denim overall pocket and wiped the warm clotty blood and bone fragments off his face. Then, using the blood-stained bat as support, he pushed himself up and walked over to his workbench. His power tools were all neatly arranged, shelf after shelf of drills, electric skill saws, and all manner and description of tools were proudly displayed.

Reaching up and using both hands to lift his heavy Stihl petrol chain saw from the top shelf, he calmly placed it down on the workbench and admired the newly sharpened teeth spread along the length of its curved blade.

As he picked it up and pulled back hard on the start cord, the trembling machine coughed to life and petrol fumes travelled the room, the white acrid smoke dispelling into the night air through the open glass skylight above. The Stihl's engine roared, but the freshly sharpened blade remained static until he engaged its single mechanical gear, and the perfectly honed blade spun to life.

The blade would slice deep into Stephan's flesh, cut through his bones like butter. Binnie wondered if this time he should start with the ankles or whether it would be better to go straight for the neck as he raised the vibrating mechanical monster above the lifeless body.

That sulphuric acid might be good stuff, but human flesh and bones take an awful lot of flushing away. I really do hope you appreciate all the hard work I put into this Mac, Binnie thought, eventually deciding he'd start with the ankles…

23. Archie

Apart from the power outage during the night, Archie's day had started just like any other. He'd reset the main switch, wondered to himself if Rebecca might have caused it, but he'd noticed workmen digging holes across the road so assumed it was either them or the ancient wiring again. And, anyway, even if Rebecca was up to something, he couldn't prove it. Enid would never believe him, so he just carried on with his habitual raking up of the leaves from the gravel drive, followed by the moving of his freshly cut logs.

Shifting them two, maybe three at a time, he stacked them neatly on the dry wood pile he was forming at the back of the shed. The only interruption to his physical exertion was occasional thoughts of Rebecca. Scratching his greying scalp, he'd stop now and then midway between the wheelbarrow and the wood pile to think.

What can I do? he asked himself. *If I say something to Enid, she won't believe me? Even if she did, what proof do I have? An old Betamax tape with four minutes and twenty seconds missing. What does that prove? Nothing. No, I need more than that. Much more.*

Archie felt for the master keys suspended on the belt of his old grey overalls, the same keys that unlocked every room in the house. And decided he'd take a sneaky look at Rebecca's room later.

"Back to work Archie," he mumbled to himself, as the driving rain beat rhythmically down on top of the single storey corrugated roof, cascading into the water butt below.

Then, just as he was placing the last log on top of the neat triangular pile, he heard a scream. It was an Enid scream.

Frantically wiping his hands down the front of his blue dungarees, he ran towards the house. The front door was slightly ajar, so he rushed through the opening and stole a quick glance up the stairs, looked down the hallway, then heard the sounds of someone sobbing from the lounge. He ran in.

Enid was on her knees with her body arched forward at the bottom of the bookshelf. The safe door was wide open above her head and she was whimpering like a chastised child. He watched as she inhaled great lung fulls of air and her chest heaved up and down as she lifted her tear-ridden face to look at his. Spittle was dripping from her lips to the carpet below, her frail hands were clenched and gnarled, her voice was desperate, her spoken words so cruel and venomous.

"It's all gone, it's all gone!" she screamed. "It's all bloody gone! Oh God Archie, what have you done?" she shrieked, offering a long wailing howl. But Archie didn't understand the question, so he moved closer with his trembling hands outstretched trying to reach out and touch his friend but stopped midway as he looked up at the open safe door and understood.

"Enid, I… I would never steal from you, you're my best friend. I love you like a sister Enid… I could never…"

Archie broke down and covered his face with his hands as Enid lifted herself up, watching as his knees buckled and he dropped to the floor. He looked up half expecting Enid to place her hands in his, as he begged her to believe him.

"Please, please Enid, believe me, I could never…"

But his only reward was a slap across the face as her diamond encrusted rings scathed a rut across his cheek.

"What the hell's going on? What's going on?" Rebecca shouted as she ran into the room. "What's happening? What's

Archie done?" Her act was flawless as she looked across at the empty safe and let out a heart-wrenching scream.

"Call the police Rebecca! Call them. Archie's stolen my money," shouted Enid. Archie didn't utter a word in defence because he couldn't, the shock was too much for him. He loved this woman, he trusted her with all his heart. But she was right to think it was him. After all he was the only other person in the house who knew the combination.

Eight-six-one-nine-five-eight.

The numbers travelled through his mind in micro-seconds repeating themselves over and over again.

Eight-six-one-nine-five-eight. How did she find out the combination? How? I've never written it down. Maybe Enid had. No, she's too smart for that. So how?

An hour later, after taking down written statements from Enid and Rebecca, the arrest was made and Archibald Reginald Cunningham, former Hong Kong Police Inspector and Metropolitan Detective Sergeant, was handcuffed and taken down to Manvers Street police station in the centre of Bath. Enid was confidently assured by Detective Sergeant David

Steele that he'd be formally charged with the theft from her home of over *two hundred and fifty thousand pounds.*

Two hundred and fifty grand! You swindling old bitch. Exactly what I'd have done mind you, thought Rebecca an hour later, laying on her bed and staring up at the ornate Victorian ceiling. The anticipated *knock* on the door resonated in her room. "It's me Rebecca. It's Enid, may I come in please?"

Rebecca instantly got up, hiding the black Betamax tape under her pillow, the one she'd stolen from Archie's shed earlier that morning.

"Yes of course Enid, come in, the doors open," Rebecca replied and a few seconds later with her usual confident stride clearly amiss Enid ambled towards Rebecca's bed and sat down, sighing loudly as she wiped a tear from her eye.

"I'm really sorry to have to say this to you Rebecca but you're going to have to leave. I really hate myself for doing this to you now, but I think I need a fresh start after all this Archie business and all that."

Thank God for that, saves me handing my notice in, thought Rebecca as she reached across and gently caressed Enid's freezing cold hands.

"But Enid, I love working here," she falsely pleaded, staring into her eyes. "I feel like part of the family here. Where am I going to go?"

Enid was clearly hating every minute of it. Rebecca was playing with her emotions using everything she had from her bottomless pit of lies and deceit.

"I'm so very sorry Rebecca," Enid said, wiping yet another tear from her eye and blowing her nose. "I've deposited three months' salary in your bank account, and I've written you an excellent reference. It's all in here," she said, handing her a white printed envelope with the words "To whom it may concern," typed in bold print across the front. The envelope was sealed, so Rebecca would be sure to steam it open before handing it over to any future employer.

Wiping a false tear from her eye, Rebecca smoothed Enid's trembling hands as she carefully prepared her next question.

"Okay Enid, don't you worry, I understand. Well sort of anyway. *Thought I'd get that bit in for effect.*

"When would you like me to leave? I mean, I can always go and stay with a friend, so it's not a problem."

Enid considered changing her mind, wondering if she was being a bit too hasty in letting her go. After all, it was Archie who'd stolen her money, not the poor girl sat in front of her stroking her hands.

Rebecca could sense the change in her, and she needed to think fast. She asked her again, but this time directed her words as more of an acceptance speech rather than a person desperate to keep her job.

"To tell you the truth Enid, I was thinking of leaving anyway. You see, my uncle from America has written to me asking if I'd like to go and visit him. He's in Pennsylvania somewhere and it just happens that he needs a carer. So, please don't feel bad. I can go and stay at my friend's flat for the time being. So, no harm done."

Rebecca was almost willing Enid to respond, to accept that her friend, Rebecca, was going to be fine and to just let her go.

"Okay, Rebecca that makes me feel a little bit better, so you are free to leave at any time. And please whatever happens be happy in America my dear. Try and meet somebody nice. Settle down and have some children."

Enid got up, gently kissed Rebecca on the cheek and slowly walked out of the room. Finally… Rebecca was free…

24. The Earls

Amanda had been hospitalised. If her father hadn't called the ambulance when he had, the doctor said she'd have been dead in a matter of hours. So, she'd been lucky. The next step was rehabilitation and Bill Blake wouldn't hesitate in paying whatever it took to make his daughter well again.

As he was going down in the lift in Bristol's Royal Infirmary, Bill found himself deep in thought as the floors whisked by. Nobody had seen hide nor hair of Stephan in weeks. He'd simply disappeared off the planet after that tramp had beaten him up. *Payback time*, Bill thought, *karma you rotten evil bastard.*

As he stepped out of the lift and looked across the busy reception, he could see the Earl brothers standing on the other side of the foyer with their arms folded. Instinctively, he felt for his mobile phone as David Earl, the bigger and more menacing one of the two, approached him.

"A word my man. Get your hands out your pockets Bill. We only want a word, nothing else." Bill looked around the foyer. It was packed with people sporting broken arms, legs and all manner of injuries. He removed his hands as instructed.

"I'm not scared of you," he said, attempting to mask his inner terror. "You got anything to say to me, you do it right here, in public," he warned him, taking a step back as Terence walked across and stood at his brother's side. A policeman completely oblivious to the situation he found himself in was standing at the far end of the reception and for a split-second Bill thought about shouting out. That thought was soon dissolved as David's deep thunderous voice washed over him like a tidal wave.

"Look, if we were going to hurt you, believe me you'd be six feet under by now. The choice is yours. If you don't want to talk to us here, we can always pay a visit to Mrs Blake. It's up to you Billy boy"

So, the way *Billy boy* saw it, he didn't really have a choice. He'd nearly lost Amanda and wasn't about to take a chance with his wife, so quickly he made up his mind.

"Go on then, what is it now! What more do you want from my family?"

"Well, you've probably heard that our little bruvver's gone missing, yeah?"

"Yes, and good riddance to the bastard!" Bill snarled, as David moved a step closer and Bill took a step back.

"Look, all we need to know is if Amanda knows anything. Has she said anything to you? I mean we can always hop in the lift and ask her ourselves, can't we bro?"

Terence confirmed his brother's threat with a slow nod and Bill knew he'd would enjoy telling them what he'd seen. He smirked and this time it was him who moved a step closer.

"I saw it all you know," he said still smirking. "Because I was there," he said boldly. "I saw a tramp smash Stephan over the head with a baseball bat, then I watched as he chucked him into the back of a van. He's probably dead by now."

Bill really enjoyed telling them that part.

"What! What van. Where? When?" both brothers asked in near perfect unison.

This just gets better and better, Bill thought as he continued.

"Well, it happened a few weeks ago. I was following Stephan, trying to find out where he was keeping Amanda. I was about to call an ambulance and the police when this old tramp attacked Stephan from behind. He was swinging a baseball bat around. It happened just outside his flat on Rodway Street. The tramp was massive. He picked Stephan's limp body up like a sack of potatoes and threw him into the back of an old Transit van."

"Transit? What colour was this transit? Quick, what fucking colour? Answer me?" Terence demanded.

"White I think, yes it was white", Bill confirmed before adding, "And the tramp had bright ginger hair."

"Binnie," both brothers immediately said looking at each other. "Binnie fuckin' Walters…"

Later that night, Binnie was doing what he always did on his day off. He was cleaning his tools and sharpening the blades on his *gadgets* as he liked to call them. He was pleased, almost proud of the way he had handled Stephan's dispatch. As far as he was concerned, it was thorough and clean, but much better than that it was professional. Binnie carried on cleaning his Stihl chainsaw as suddenly the dim fluorescent light above his head flickered on and off. He looked up at the ceiling, then behind him.

"Binnie... good old Binnie Walters," said David Earl as he stepped out from the shadows holding a huge silver .357 Magnum revolver in front of him.

"What the fuck?" Binnie shouted and instantly reached across the bench towards a tin box that contained his .38 special. The one he always kept handy in case of situations like these.

But he was a bit too slow. David tutted and shot Binnie in his right kneecap. The thunderous roar of the gun exploding in such a confined space caused a box of nails to fall from the shelf at exactly the same time as Binnie's body dropped to the floor.

"You bastards, bastards!" Binnie shouted as he writhed around on the floor in agony. Terence walked over, picked up a ball pane hammer and smashed it down into his right knee, well the spot where Binnie's right knee used to be.

The brothers watched him squirming around in agony on the floor, struggling to control their eagerness to just finish him off, but they had agreed that Binnie's dispatch needed to be slow and painful and, more importantly, they wanted to know who had ordered the hit.

Terence, who hadn't said a word up until then, shook Binnie by the shoulders. Binnie was crying in pain and tears were running down his face. Fresh blood was soiling his bright ginger hair. He was trying to say something, but he couldn't.

"Tell you what Binnie," Terence said. "I'll make a deal with you. We'll make this quick, a bullet in the back of the head and it'll be all over. Just tell us who ordered the hit, then it's night-time for you. If not, me and David will stay up all night and take you apart piece by fuckin' piece, won't we David?" David poked the pointy end of the huge Magnum into Binnie's groin giving Binnie a clue as to where they'd start.

"Who grassed me up," Binnie shouted, letting out a slow agonising moan as he tried to sit up on his elbows. "Who grassed on me. Tell me…!" he screamed.

"Never mind who grassed you up, you're dead whatever happens, so just answer the fuckin' question! Who ordered the hit?" David asked, prodding the blood-soaked gristle on what was left of Binnie's knee using the barrel of the gun.

Binnie knew he didn't stand a chance. He'd been lapse and he was paying the price. He'd thought about killing all three of the bastards at the same time. But now wasn't the time to reflect. So, he made a choice and mentioned just one name as he slumped back in resignation. "McDermott," he said.

Binnie's reward was to spend the next eight or nine hours drifting in and out of consciousness while the brothers cut off his toes one by one using blunt pliers, pulled out his teeth, before finally sawing his penis off with his own hacksaw. Binnie Walters was the legend that was – but was no more.

Andy McDermott was going to be next…

25. Christi

"*Knock, knock.*"

"Come in," said DCI Karen Cook as Christi popped her head around the door.

"Hi guv, you got a minute?" she asked. "There's something I need to talk to you about. You busy?"

"A bit but take a seat Christi. I've got few minutes before I dash off to court and testify against that lying prick, Mark Cooper. He thought it would be funny to change his plea at the last minute, so I'm giving evidence. Anyway, never mind about that now. Sit down, what's on your mind?"

Christi sat down on the chair opposite, shuffling awkwardly on her seat before beginning her report. Karen closed her file.

"Well guv, I thought I'd take a look at what McDermott got up to on his nights off and it's really bloody interesting. Not only has he just bought himself a new car, and I might add a BMW at that, he's also bought himself a posh new flat up on the Downs and he's regularly entertaining a young lady visitor. Now take a wild guess who that visitor might be."

"Rebecca Thorneycroft by any chance?" DCI Cook answered almost rhetorically.

"Right first-time guv. Rebecca bloody Thorneycroft."

Christi, although desperate to tell her the rest, sat back in her chair for a moment allowing Karen her own thoughts. And they weren't long in coming.

"Still not enough though is it Christi? I mean, what does that prove? A posh flat, a new bit of floozy, they'd just laugh us out of court."

Christi sat forward and turned to the next page of her report, knowing full well that Karen would really appreciate this part.

"No, you're dead right guv, it's not enough. But when you add to the equation that yet another of her ex-employers a Wilf Kennedy has just died of a heart attack whilst in her care, it starts to get really bloody interesting."

Karen immediately picked the phone up on her desk and dialled. "Cancel my court appearance today will you Sergeant... Yes, yes, I know but something more important than Mark bloody Cooper nicking a few dozen cars has come up."

Karen replaced the phone without waiting for the Sergeant's response. She sat forward in her seat. "I'm all ears Christi, go on."

Christi smiled knowing her guvnor would just love what was coming next.

"Well, it gets even better because Thorneycroft's last employer, A Mrs uh." Christi looked down at her file. "A Mrs Enid Williams has just had over two hundred and fifty grand nicked out of her safe and some poor old ex-copper has been charged with the theft. Now, is it me, or do a lot of things seem to happen every time this Thorneycroft woman enters the fray?"

Christi allowed the question to hang in the air as Karen drummed her pen on the desk deep in thought.

"Right, bring her in," Karen said after a few moments of deliberation. "Don't bring her here though. Take her down to Bridewell and lock her up in a cell well out of the way. We've got twenty-four hours before we need to apply for an extension, so let's pick her up now. McDermott can't know anything about this. Not yet. I'll sign the arrest warrant myself."

"Okay guv. Who's going be the interviewing officer?" Christi asked, hoping it was going to be her. "I mean, I know it's not on our patch, it's a Bath investigation. But I'd love to watch the bitch squirm. I've already called Manvers Street and had a little chat with the arresting officer."

Christi held up the file and read from her notes. "I spoke to a Detective Sergeant David Steele and he told me this Archie Cunningham, the one they've charged with the theft, is an ex-copper with an unblemished record. He's not even got a speeding ticket against him. But, according to Mrs Williams, Cunningham was the only one apart from her who knew the combination to the safe. There wasn't any evidence of forced entry. His prints were all over the dial."

"Now this is where it gets even more interesting, because in his statement he said he had proof that it was Thorneycroft who'd nicked it. It was on a security tape he'd installed in the hall cupboard. And guess what guv?"

"Go on."

"The tape's gone missing."

"Then Thorneycroft must have it," Karen quickly responded.

"Exactly."

"Okay guv, who's doing the interview?" Christi asked her again, still hoping it was her.

"McDermott's going to do it," Karen calmly replied. "You just keep him out of the way for now. We don't want him getting too jumpy, do we? Not yet. Let's just sit back and watch the snake try and wiggle out of this one."

Christi sniffed. Even she hadn't thought of that one…

26. Rebecca

"Rebecca Thorneycroft… are you Miss Rebecca Thorneycroft," the tall man asked, holding out his warrant card and saying his name was Detective Sergeant David Steele of the Avon and Somerset Constabulary.

"Yes, yes, that's me," Rebecca nervously replied before asking, "What's this all about?"

"I'd like you to accompany me down to Bridewell police station. It's nothing to worry about, we just need to clear up a few things. I can arrest you if necessary, but I was rather hoping you'd come with us of your own free will."

Rebecca was terrified, and gripped hold of her Prada handbag and placed it under her arm as car after car continually whooshed passed with driver's rubber necking as the police car's flashing lights brought attention to the scene.

The Woman Police Constable in the driver's seat offered Rebecca a knowing smile through the windscreen, like she'd been caught shoplifting. Not that Rebecca ever had, but to her that's how it felt.

"Okay it seems as though I don't have much of a choice, do I? Rebecca replied in a calmer tone. "So, let's get it over and done with. This is the second time you've done this to me. I'm getting pissed off with it now," Rebecca said as the Sergeant customarily pushed her head down onto the back seat.

"I'll take that," he said, taking possession of her handbag before slamming the car door shut and getting in the front.

Sergeant Steele turned around in the front seat and faced her.

"Before we get going, I need to read you your rights Rebecca," he said as she froze and gripped the edge of her seat "What? What have I done?"

But Sergeant Steel ignored her question and started to read. "Rebecca Susan Thorneycroft, I am arresting you on suspicion of the murders of a Mrs Mae Wilson and a Mr Wilfred Kennedy. You are also being placed under arrest on the suspicion of the theft of two hundred and fifty thousand pounds in cash from a house owned by a Mrs Enid Williams. You do not have to say anything, but it may harm your defence if you do not mention when questioned something which you might later rely on in court. Anything you do say now may be given in evidence."

The journey down to Bridewell took less than eight or nine minutes. The WPC switched on the blue's and twos to cut through the heavy afternoon traffic on Park Street.

"So, do I need a solicitor?" Rebecca asked, as usual faking naivety from the back of the car.

"All that will be explained to you at the station Miss Thorneycroft. You haven't been charged as yet, but my advice would be to say as little as possible before you have a chat with your solicitor."

Right Symes. Time to earn your keep.

The car drove around the back, through the big iron gates that closed electrically behind her and parked in front of an ominous looking blue door at the rear. The Sergeant immediately got out and Rebecca shuddered as he demanded, "Come on then, get out, out!"

Rebecca got out, the WPC instantly taking hold of her arm near the elbow as she looked up at the razor wire that coiled a loop along the top of the tall perimeter fence. She was led through an off-white metal door which made a strange buzzing noise, before being marched along a bleak corridor with green vinyl floor tiles and grim looking cell doors set either side.

Reaching the far end, she was led through yet another door and standing on other side was a desk Sergeant who looked ominously down at her from behind a counter so tall that it almost reached her chin.

"Oh, what a lovely surprise," he scowled. "What have you got for me today Sergeant Steele?" were the Sergeant's first words as he leant over the desk looking her up and down, admiring her form.

Without answering, and almost robotically, Sergeant Steele started to read out her name, age, her last known address and the reason for her arrest from his notepad. The desk Sergeant, clearly unimpressed and without looking up, breathed out heavily through his nose as he scribbled something down on a notepad behind the desk, before handing it to Rebecca.

"Sign this please and make sure you tick all the boxes."

The WPC's grasp was finally released, and she read the piece of paper. It asked the usual things – Did she have any serious illnesses that might require the attendance of a doctor? Was she allergic to anything? Was she on any medication? Did she have suicidal thoughts? The last question stuck in her mind more than the others as she ticked the boxes and signed the form. The WPC then handed the Sergeant Rebecca's handbag.

"Is there anything I should be worried about in here," the Sergeant asked, looking at her ominously.

"No, only some make-up, a set of keys and a couple of credit cards I think," Rebecca nonchalantly replied, looking around at the wanted posters and warning notices in the bleak looking room.

"Good, have you anything on your person that you could use to endanger yourself or those around you."

"No."

"Okay, last question Miss Thorneycroft. Are you currently in possession of, or have you taken any drugs of any kind in the last twenty-four hours? By that I mean Class A, Class B, prescription or otherwise."

"No!" Rebecca confirmed, shouting out her answer.

"Good," said the Sergeant, calmly emptying the contents of her handbag onto the counter. "In that case, take her to cell four," he shouted at the top of his voice. The uniformed WPC took her by the arm and led her back down the bleak corridor.

The officer unlocked the cell door and waited as Rebecca walked in ahead then, as soon as they were in, she asked her to "Remove your shoes and your belt if you are wearing one." Before brusquely informing her that she would be carrying out a thorough search of her pockets and that would involve her removing all her clothing, including her underwear, so they could be sent for forensic analysis. She then went on to inform her that the procedure was both legal and mandatory, and it was within her rights to request a second officer to be in attendance while it was carried out.

"So, would you like a second officer present, Miss Thorneycroft?" she asked, pulling on a pair of see through silica gloves and pulling out a large white bag from her pocket with the words *forensic evidence* written on the front.

The officer's stoic look hadn't altered the whole time she'd been talking to her. There was no sign of emotion at all, not an, "Are you okay?" and not even a "Do you need anything?" Nothing, she just coldly stared at Rebecca.

Rebecca was wearing a white flowery top and black pencil skirt. She didn't answer the question. Instead, she demanded to see a solicitor. The officer wasn't fazed and simply nodded and confirmed that it was within her rights to contact a solicitor, but only once her clothes had been removed and sent away for forensic analysis.

"What is the name of your solicitor and where are they based?" the officer enquired still without any outward emotion.

"His name is Mr Dominic Symes and the firm are called Montague and Syme's. They are based in Clifton."

"Okay, as soon as we're done here, I'll ask the desk Sergeant to call him," she replied, pushing the cell door closed with the heel of her foot creating a loud *bang*!

Around about the same time, McDermott received a call from DCI Karen Cook at Redland police station.

"Hi Andy, where are you at the moment?" Karen enquired, knowing full well he was either in his car smoking, or drinking alcohol in some seedy bar somewhere. But Karen was wrong. McDermott was sitting in a travel agency in Yate booking a surprise holiday to Tenerife for Rebecca and himself.

"I really need to take this," he informed the lady behind the desk as he placed his hand over the phone and walked outside, coughing to clear his throat.

"I'm on my way in guv," he declared before she had a chance to ask him where he was. "I had a flat tyre this morning. I'll be with you in about…" Andy looked down at his watch. "In about half an hour guv. What's up?"

"I need you to divert down to Bridewell Andy," Karen told him. "I want you to question a prisoner we have in custody. The case file's already down there with the desk Sergeant. Make sure you have a good look at it before you start the interview."

"Course guv. I'll get down there straight away," Andy replied, wondering why she'd asked him rather than one of the local Detectives. But, before he could ask, Karen abruptly cut him off and answered it for him.

"I'm asking you because it's somebody you've already met. It's a woman by the name of… let me see now… ah, here we are, her name's Rebecca Thorneycroft. I think you interviewed her off the record in Bath a while back. Do you remember her?"

McDermott nearly dropped the phone as people walked past left and right in the busy shopping centre. He stood open mouthed, completely poleaxed, frightened out of his skin. He couldn't respond to Karen's question because at that juncture words just failed him.

"Andy are you still there?" Karen asked. She placed her hand over the phone and looked across the desk at Christi who was trying extremely hard to contain an outburst of laughter. "Yes, guv I'm still here," he nervously replied. "I'll be there in about half an hour."

Rebecca was inside her cell, sat on a thin blue plastic mattress staring at the drab grey blockwork walls covered in all manner of gang related graffiti and messages. One of them stood out above the rest and read, "Give up all hope all ye who enter here. I just got life!"

Rebecca shuddered, recognising the quote from *Dante Alighieri's Inferno*. She'd read the poem in one of the childrens' homes she was in at the time. But for the life of her she couldn't remember which one.

She dropped her head into her hands and ran her fingers through her jet-black hair, sighing as she looked across at the filthy stainless-steel toilet in the corner wondering why it didn't have a seat. The thin blue smock she wore smelt of washing powder and starch as she sat for a few minutes looking around the bleak cell. The only light was from a thin dust covered fluorescent tube encased in rusty steel mesh hanging high above her head.

She could hear raised angry voices in the corridor. It sounded like a scuffle was taking place outside. Then the banging started, and the whole corridor erupted as prisoner after prisoner shouted from one cell to another and began banging their fists on the heavy cell doors.

She was utterly terrified and put her fingers in her ears. She felt vulnerable, alone again, just like the sad little girl she used to be when Tom would leave her all alone while he entertained his so-called lady friends or was out burglarising some poor unsuspecting family home.

The noise seemed to quell as she heard the sound of keys rattling in the big brass lock, and the huge cell door suddenly swung open. In walked Sergeant Steele holding a portable phone in his hand.

"You wanted to speak to a solicitor," he said handing her the small black telephone. "Well he's on the line."

Rebecca immediately got to her feet and took the phone. The Sergeant turned his back to her, stared at the flickering fluorescent light, pretending he wasn't listening to the conversation. Rebecca knew he was.

"Hello, is that you Mr Symes?" she asked in an unusually polite tone.

"Yes, it's me Rebecca, replied Symes, letting a loud drawn out sigh. Then, before she could say anything, he said, "Now listen to me very carefully Rebecca. Do not! And I repeat do not say a word to anyone. Not even to me on this telephone. I will be there within the hour. Remember, not a word to anyone. Goodbye."

And that was that. The line went dead and its dull monotonous tone echoed in the concrete confines of the eight by six-foot cell. Sergeant Steele looked around.

"All done then. That was short and sweet," he quipped as he retrieved the phone.

"Yes, all done," Rebecca replied, feeling a little more confident now that Symes was on his way, despite his gruffness on the phone. *Mind you*, she thought, *if I'm going down, he's going down with me.*

"So, what happens next?" she asked, as the Sergeant began to close the door.

"Well, you'll be interviewed under caution by a Sergeant McDermott from Redland police station," he confirmed as he checked his watch. "He should be here any minute now." Then he looked back, smiled and slammed the cell door behind him. Rebecca wasn't smiling…

27. McDermott

McDermott's new BMW 330i rushed through the back gates of Bridewell police headquarters. The gates slowly slid across slamming themselves shut behind him. Swiping his plastic card, he opened the outside door and paced down the corridor passed the cells, including the one holding Rebecca. Reaching the far end, he opened the door and a less than happy Sergeant Steele greeted him.

"Well, look what the cat's dragged in. I heard you were coming over. Bit out of order though isn't it? After all it was me who made the arrest."

There was no love lost between the two Sergeants. Steele was a Johnny upright bobby and straight as a dye. And, put simply, McDermott wasn't. His drink and drugs reputation preceded him. So, their relationship or rather the lack of it was like a feral cat might experience with a dog.

"Just cut out the crap and hand me the file will you Steele," McDermott said, eyeing his fellow officer up and down with a look of disdain. Steele didn't bother to reply. He just tossed the file across the desk before walking out and slamming the station's front door behind him.

McDermott sighed, breathed out and shook his head as he looked at the all too familiar face of Rebecca staring straight back at him. He had an idea, one that he'd been mulling over during the drive over. He knew the rules, so was fully aware that they could only keep her in custody for a maximum of twenty-four hours. After that, they would need to apply through the court for an extension of seventy-two hours or be forced to release her without charge.

All he had to do was throw a sicky, take a few days out and that way somebody else would have to do the interview. Knowing Rebecca like he did, they wouldn't find out a bloody thing. After all, they had no credible evidence, nothing that would stand up in court. And, so what if he was shagging a suspect. He didn't know anything about little old ladies being robbed or a stack of gold coins going missing. So, the enemy were close, but they weren't over the walls yet.

He knew the camera behind the desk was recording his every move. He put the file back on the desk, collapsed to the floor and began to writhe around in agony holding his chest as the desk Sergeant looked down in horror. "Quick! Quick, phone an ambulance, McDermott's collapsed," the Sergeant shouted as the WPC ran from behind the counter.

Less than an hour later DCI Karen Cook received a telephone call at Redland police station informing her that Detective Sergeant Andrew McDermott had been admitted to the Bristol Royal Infirmary with a suspected heart attack.

Karen nearly threw the phone across the office as she realised McDermott might live to fight another day.

Or at least that's what she thought…

28. Rebecca

The cell door swung open and in walked Christi Blake with DCI Karen Cook two steps behind her. Rebecca was finishing off the remnants of a McDonald's burger and chips, courtesy of HM Prison Service. The heavy cell door banged shut behind them as they both stood in the centre of the cell watching Rebecca nonchalantly licking tomato sauce from her fingers.

"Rebecca Thorneycroft," Karen stated. "You have been brought in for questioning in relation to two suspected murders and on the suspicion of assisting, or taking part in, the theft of over two hundred and fifty thousand pounds from the house of the late Enid Williams of Lonsdale. Do you have anything to say?"

"So, she's dead, then is she? Rebecca asked. "That's really sad." *One less witness to worry about*, she thought as Christi quickly responded.

"Mrs Williams passed away in her sleep three nights ago, no doubt brought on by the thought of her life savings being robbed from under her Miss Thorneycroft!"

"Miss Thorneycroft, we are here to inform you that your solicitor, Mr Dominic Symes, is here to see you in the interview room." Karen looked at her watch. "It is now exactly one thirty in the afternoon and you have precisely thirty minutes. After your meeting with Mr Symes, Detective Inspector Blake and I will interview you in connection with these allegations. Do you have anything else to say?"

She didn't, so continued chewing on the remnants of her burger and chips, deep in thought.

That's six hours gone already. Where's McDermott? she thought but knew better than to ask. Although Karen wished she would.

"No, I have nothing to say," she eventually replied.

"In that case, you'll be handcuffed and taken down to the interview room."

Rebecca immediately offered out her wrists in what seemed to Karen like a far too practiced manner as Christi snapped the cuffs shut and led her out of the cell.

As she entered room *eight*, Christi told her to sit down in the chair in the opposite corner. Two large tape machines sat ominously on the table opposite with four wooden-backed chairs parked either side. There was a knock at the door. Christi opened it and in walked Symes with his thick brown leather briefcase neatly tucked under his right arm. If she hadn't known better, she could have sworn he looked almost cheerful as he placed it down on the table. She was more than aware that Symes was a very deeply troubled and an extremely worried man.

"Okay Detectives, the time now is exactly one thirty-five in the afternoon," Symes confidently announced. "So, if you would be so kind, I would like to talk to my client in private."

Karen and Christi both looked at each other and nodded in unison as Christi calmly opened the door and they left the room. Symes sat down at the desk and started to write something down. Then he handed Rebecca a sheet of full-scap paper with the words, *"Don't say anything. Let me direct the questions. Just either nod or shake your head in response."*

Rebecca read it, nodded in confirmation, then reached across for the pad and pen. *Can you contact my friend, a Mr Paul Smart? He runs a bar called Gee Gees on the Costa Nova in Javea, Spain. Can you ask him to get on the next flight out?*

He'll know where to stash my money. I've got it put away. But if they find it, we're both FUCKED!!

"Yes, Miss Thorneycroft, leave that to me," Symes confirmed as Rebecca handed the pad back. Then, looking over the top of his gold rimmed spectacles, he said, "These are extremely serious allegations being made against you. Are they well founded or are you innocent of all charges?"

Rebecca fought the urge to blurt out that Symes' knew damn well she wasn't bloody innocent. But didn't.

"I'll take that as an innocent plea then Miss Thorneycroft," said Symes, pointing at the pad and holding his finger to his lips intermating further silence.

"Okay, it is my understanding that the original interviewing officer, a Detective by the name of… let me see now," he said faking a glance at the file. "Ah here it is, it was going to be a Detective by the name of Sergeant Andrew McDermott but unfortunately he's unable to attend. The Sergeant on the desk has informed me that he has been taken to hospital with a suspected heart attack."

Rebecca couldn't help but punch the air in silence as Symes wrote down another note. A longer one this time. *We need to play the time game here. From what I can gather, they have no real evidence against you and they only have another sixteen hours to either charge or release you. They can apply through the local magistrate for an extension, but if you remain silent, I think I can get you released.*

For the first time since her arrest, Rebecca could see the hope written in Symes' scribbled lines and wondered if she might have underestimated him. Symes looked at his watch. It was exactly two o'clock in the afternoon. He reached across, retrieved the pad, ripped the first three pages up and placed them in his briefcase.

"You are now going to be interviewed by both the lady officers, but don't worry I will be sat right next to you the whole time. By law, you are entitled to refreshments during the interview such as glass of water or a cup of tea. Would you like me to arrange that for you Miss Thorneycroft?"

"No, thank you, Mr Symes," she said as Symes rose from the chair, knocked on the security window and a few moments later the door opened and standing in the corridor were Karen and Christi.

"My client is ready for your questions now, Symes informed them, before adding, "My client has declined any refreshment at this stage. But then cheekily added, "If it's not too much trouble, mine is a black coffee with two sugars."

Karen was inwardly livid, but she knew the rules like the back of her hand. She cleverly she rose to the challenge by sarcastically adding, "Call the desk Sergeant will you DI Blake to arrange that. No doubt Mr Symes here would like a few biscuits with it?"

Symes thought better than to push it any further. He retreated back into the room and sat down opposite both of the officers. Karen told Rebecca to sit down and pulled out a large blue file with her photograph stapled to the front. Christi broke the seals on two identical audio tapes before placing them in the machine while reading out the time, date and Rebecca's full name and address.

"Also present in the room are Detective Chief Inspector Karen Cook, collar number 28019, of the Avon and Somerset Constabulary who is leading the investigation together with myself, Detective Inspector Christine Blake, collar number 27167, of the Avon and Somerset Constabulary. Sat opposite is Miss Rebecca Susan Thorneycroft who is being detained on suspicion of two counts of murder and one count of theft of two hundred and fifty thousand pounds in cash."

"Representing Miss Thorneycroft is her solicitor, a Mr Dominic Symes of Montague Symes & Co, from Clifton Bristol. The interview will now commence."

Karen leant over the desk. She spread out pictures of Wilf, Aunt Mae and Enid Williams in front of Rebecca and asked if she recognised any of them. Symes nodded in the affirmative that she could answer.

"Yes, they are all former employers of mine," Rebecca confirmed.

"You say *former* Rebecca," Karen said instantly cutting in. "Former only because they are all dead! Bit of a coincidence that don't you think, seeing as you were working for two of them when they died?"

Rebecca was about to reply when Symes held his hand up to cut her off. "I advise my client not to answer that question," he said firmly.

Rebecca smiled, Symes was really coming into his own, *maybe he was worth the twenty-five grand*, she thought as

Christi sat forward. "Okay Miss Thorneycroft do you deny that you are, or were, having a relationship with one of our officers, namely a Detective Sergeant Andrew McDermott of the Avon and Somerset Constabulary? The same officer that interviewed you in connection with an inheritance you received from one of your *former* employers. In this particular case, the late Mrs Enid Williams."

Rebecca remained quiet. Symes didn't, however.

"I advise my client not to answer that question and I might remind the officers that what my client does in her spare time is her own business and nobody else's. I would like that last question struck from the record as it bears no actual relevance to the current case."

Symes was on fire and Karen was becoming more and more annoyed and literally spat out, "So, Mr Symes, what questions will you allow your client to answer?" "And on that note wasn't it your company who were employed to carry out the reading on behalf of the late Mrs Williams' estate."

Symes didn't flinch or even bat an eyelid at the intimation that he'd been somehow complicit in the forging of the will.

He simply answered Karen's question, "A pure coincidence, Clifton is a very small place."

Christi cut in again, "I think there's been far too many coincidences Mr Symes. In fact, I propose that Miss Thorneycroft here, aided I might add by Detective Sergeant Andrew McDermott have been working together and are very much involved in the death of her former employers. And, right at this moment, we are applying to the magistrate for the exhumation of Mrs Mae Wilson's body in order to carry out a full autopsy so that we can establish the real cause of her death!"

The tide had suddenly turned, and Rebecca was fighting to stop herself from being physically sick. Even the previously confident, *on fire* Symes let out a gasp at the news that dear old Aunt Mae's body was going to be exhumed. The atmosphere in the room turned electric and you could cut it with a blunt butter knife as Christi carried on.

"We are also applying to the magistrate for an extension of your arrest for a further seventy-two hours on the basis that it will allow enough time to exhume Mrs Wilson's body and carry out an autopsy. Have you any questions?"

Symes certainly did and immediately cut in.

"In that case, I would like a full copy of the case file on my desk within the next eight hours as is my client's right under clause number…"

Karen fired back, "We are fully aware of your client's rights under the current law Mr Symes! We anticipated such a request so you can have this one."

Karen slammed the case the file down on the desk informing him, "So, that seems to wrap things up rather nicely. The prisoner will now be escorted back to her holding cell and this interview is terminated at precisely three fifteen."

Christi then pushed the two eject buttons on the tape machine and placed the two sealed tapes into separate brown envelopes.

"May I request a few moments alone with my client?" Symes asked. "My original time was cut short by a good four minutes earlier," he said, looking over his spectacles at his watch.

Both Christi and Karen nodded in the affirmative and, as they were leaving the room, Karen brusquely added, "Five minutes and that's all." The heavy door swung shut with a loud *thud* as Rebecca glared at Symes. "Is that it then?" she asked. "I mean is that all you've got to say Symes. My bloody neck is on the line here and I've no need to remind you that..."

Symes immediately held up his hand and cut her off, making a *shushing* sound with his finger indicating that she should be quiet.

"Rebecca, for your own sake please be quiet," he said in less than a whisper. "Calm yourself down. As soon as I leave here, I'm going straight back to my office to prepare your case, so stop worrying because unless Sergeant McDermott decides to do a plea bargain and turn Queen's evidence you don't have a case to answer. In my opinion, they don't have any real evidence against you because if they had we'd have seen it by now. So, let them dig her up," he said defiantly, still talking in less than a whisper. "Who's to say it was you?"

Symes raised his eyebrows and Rebecca swallowed hard...

29. Pauly (Moo) Smart

Pauly Smart was affectionately known as *Pauly Moo* and was the type of person you could rely on. He'd been christened Pauly Moo by Rebecca after playing the front end of a cow in a performance that the childrens' home had put on for harvest festival.

Pauly was the only male friend Rebecca had ever really trusted. He was one of the few in the home that didn't ask her for sexual favours and had fought her corner on more than one occasion. So, in simple terms, Pauly was Rebecca's best friend and in turn she absolutely adored him. Way back in the early days while laying on her dormitory bed, she'd dream of the day she walked up the aisle with him, arm in arm. Pauly was her soulmate.

Pauly's parents had given him up for adoption after he'd been diagnosed with *dissociative identity disorder*, or in plain terms a split personality. And like all sufferers, the disorder came and went as it pleased, and the *victim* was left completely unaware of having suffered a bout, or an *episode* as the doctors described it.

All childrens' homes had what they termed access to a "sin bin" – a room where the so-say *naughty* children were sent and Pendleton Childrens' Home was no different. Their room was simply called room eight and this was where Pauly would spend his time completely unaware of where he was, or even indeed who he was. He would be sent to room eight after adopting alter ego's that came and went as they pleased. But it was when Pauly became Gilbert that he was at his most dangerous, and the personality the staff at Pendleton feared the most.

You see Gilbert could be spitefully cruel and, above all, violent and greedy. In effect, Gilbert was everything the real Pauly Moo wasn't. On the occasions when Gilbert arrived, the staff wouldn't place him in room eight. Instead he'd be sent straight to a padded cell for his own protection.

From day one, Rebecca had never experienced anything strange or odd about him. Pauly would simply disappear for a few days then re-appear as though nothing had happened. To her, he was always the same – bright, funny, loyal and above all extremely kind. But Rebecca's feelings changed the day she'd walked into Pauly's room and found him in a rather uncompromising sexual entanglement with another boy.

Discovering completely by accident Pauly's penchant or shall we say *love for other men.* She was dumbstruck and utterly heartbroken. For four days she did nothing but lay on her bed alone openly weeping, before finally, and after Pauly begging her for forgiveness, she finally accepted that this was who he was meant to be. And the man standing at the end of her bed pleading to be forgiven was the same Pauly Moo that would always protect her, guide her and primarily love her. Following her untimely arrest, Rebecca realised she needed help. And Pauly Moo was exactly where she'd seek it.

Pauly was busy mixing a *Manhattan* cocktail for a German patron as the phone rang in *Gee-Gee's* bar. He owned *Gee Gees* jointly with his husband, Brett, and it was set just above the busy Spanish resort of Javea on Spain's sunny Costa Blanca.

"Hello, *Gee-Gees*, Pauly speaking, how can I help you?"

"Is that Mr Paul Smart?" the voice asked.

"Yes, yes, it is, how can I help you?" Pauly asked.

"My name is Dominic Symes. I am a solicitor currently representing a client by the name of Miss Rebecca Thorneycroft. I understand that you and she are close friends?"

"We are," Pauly blurted out. "What's happened? Is she all right?"

"Yes, yes she's fine Mr Smart," Symes quickly confirmed. "But I'm sorry to say she is in a spot of trouble, and I'm afraid…"

"What sort of trouble?" Pauly demanded. "Oh my God…" he said, pressing the phone closer to his ear.

"Mr Smart will you please let me finish and stop interrupting me! I don't have very long and I need you to listen to me very carefully."

"Sorry, I'm just upset…. please carry on."

Pauly was close to tears as his husband placed a reassuring arm around his shoulder, allowing Symes to resume his conversation.

"Rebecca has been arrested on suspicion of a double murder and the theft of two hundred and fifty thousand pounds in cash.

She is, of course, completely innocent of all charges but has asked me to contact you to see if you are able to fly back as soon as possible to discuss shall we say, "certain arrangements concerning her finances". She asked me to tell you she loves you and she wants you to know you are the only person she can really trust."

Pauly looked at his watch. The time was exactly eight in the evening and all the Ryanair and easyJet flights would be fully booked. It would have to be tomorrow.

"Mr Symes…" Pauly replied. "Mr Symes, please tell Rebecca I'll be on the first flight into Bristol tomorrow morning… Oh, and Mr Symes, please make sure nothing happens to her in the meantime, okay."

Pauly meant it. You only upset Pauly at your peril…

30. McDermott

Bristol's Royal Infirmary was an extremely efficient and well-run hospital but, like all hospitals, it could be a lonely sanctum where you lay day after day staring at the walls waiting for the doctor's rounds. In normal circumstances, any patient worth his salt would be hoping to be discharged.

But in McDermott's case, he was taken there hoping for the complete opposite. He wanted to stay. He felt safe within the confines of its starched white walls. The only visitors he'd received in the last twenty-four hours were his daughter, Karen and Sergeant Tanner, the recently retired desk Sergeant from Redland police station.

During the past eight hours, they'd carried out every test known to medical science. But nobody knew better than he that there was absolutely nothing wrong with him. So, he prayed they'd keep him in for observation at least. But hospital beds were few and far between. He waited and, an hour later, he was woken by a voice at the end of the bed.

"Mr McDermott?" the doctor asked as the nurse wrapped the privacy screen around.

"Yes, that's me," McDermott replied, sitting up and folding his arms across his chest. "So, what's the verdict then doc? Am I going to croak it?"

"No, Mr McDermott, you certainly are not going to croak it! the doctor replied, clearly annoyed at his nonchalant attitude at the way he'd described his own death.

"In fact, for a man of your age, a smoker and a drinker to boot, you are in incredibly good health. You do have rather high cholesterol, but we can deal with that as an outpatient using medication. But I'm glad to report that you are in perfectly good health. Your cardiac test showed no abnormalities whatsoever. So, you are free to go home Mr McDermott. You are formally discharged."

The doctor handed the nurse a piece of paper he tore from a pad and stood for a moment at the end of the bed. This wasn't good news at all for McDermott. He needed more time, especially since Sergeant Tanner had just told him that Rebecca was going to be held in custody for another seventy-two hours.

Then relief set in as the doctor added, "However, I am recommending you take complete rest. I see you are a

Detective Sergeant in the CID. Well one can only imagine what stresses and strains that must put on you. So, you need to take at least a month off before returning to work."

A month, no stress, no interview, nothing. Then it's over, they'll have to release her by then.

"Thanks for the advice doctor. I'll be certain to take you up on that," McDermott cheerfully announced, resting his head back on the cold pillow as an inner calmness started to overcome him.

That was until the privacy screen was pulled back and stood in front of him like two hunting dogs were DCI Karen Cook and beside her DI Christi Blake.

"Thought we'd pop in and see how you're getting on Sergeant," Karen cheerfully announced as she moved closer to the bed. Christi had placed the *Sun* newspaper and a bunch of grapes on his bedside cabinet.

"According to the doctor, it seems you're going to pull through after all. Bit worrying though don't you think. I mean a middle-aged man, a smoker, drinker and a bloody baby snatcher who just happens to be shagging one of our prime suspects, that must take its toll on a person's body."

McDermott sat bolt upright in bed knowing full well the game was up but, like all copper's – even bent ones, he knew his rights. "Look, unless I am under caution or you are going to charge me with something, I suggest you both go back to what you do best – snooping into other peoples' business. I had nothing to do with any of Rebecca's business goings on and the fact that I have been seeing her doesn't prove anything at all."

Christi cut in, "No you're dead right Sergeant, it doesn't prove anything, but you've just confirmed to us that you are having a relationship with a prime suspect in a prominent murder investigation, and that on its own is enough to have you suspended prior to further investigation. So, enjoy the rest of your time off because as of this moment you are suspended from duty. Make sure you hand over your warrant card at Redland police station within an hour of your release."

Christi sniffed, that gave her great satisfaction. But Karen was trying to hide any obvious outward amusement as they were very close to wrapping up two high profile murder investigations and the theft of over two hundred and fifty thousand pounds in cash. So, without exchanging another word, they both walked back down the ward towards the exit as McDermott reached across to his locker, pulled out his clothes and started to dress.

Outside the BRI, the sun was breaking through the grey clouds above, a light breeze was running up and down Marlborough Street as a constant stream of traffic rushed up and down. McDermott quickened his pace and walked across the crossing hoping to find a taxi at the bottom of Earl Street.

As he walked further down the hill, he got the impression he was being followed, but wasn't sure if his mind was playing tricks on him after meeting the two Rottweilers earlier.

He picked up his step once more and, just as he was approaching the bottom of the hill, a black BMW 440 convertible screeched to a halt with two hooded men sat in the front. McDermott instinctively ducked into a shop doorway and started banging and rattling the door, but the shop hadn't been open for several years and the door wouldn't budge.

Trapped in the doorway, he looked around as the two hoodies got out of the car and stood in the opening, blocking his exit. The taller of the two was the first to speak.

"Mac, isn't it? Binnie used to call you that didn't he? Well me and my bro here would like a little chat with you Mac. You know, sort of off the record."

McDermott was absolutely terrified. His thoughts soon ignited a trail of fresh urine running the length of his legs before puddling for a moment then forming a line down the hill. He tried to run, to get out, but the Earls blocked his way and one of them lashed out at him with a heavy punch just below the groin causing him to double over in pain and fall down into the shop doorway.

The second attack was much more frenzied as both brothers repeatedly punched and kicked out until he lay mired in his own vomit and blood.

Suddenly, as fast as it had started it stopped, and two sets of arms pulled McDermott's blood-soaked body to his feet and shoved him into the back of the car. Strangely enough, and probably because of the awareness course he'd attended during police training, all McDermott could think about was how ironic it was that the Earls had kidnapped him in broad daylight, in a place called *Earl Street*.

The shock caused adrenaline to pump through his damaged frame at an alarming rate but, doing what it did best, soothing his seven broken teeth, five cracked ribs and the detached retina he'd attained. Total fear set in engulfing him to the point where he couldn't scream out anymore. His mouth opened then closed, but not a sound came out. He heard the large engine roar as the car drove smoothly away on its one-way journey to a destination as yet unknown...

31. McDermott

Karen placed Rebecca's Crown Prosecution Service file down in front of her and looked across at the clock, letting out a loud sigh. It was a few minutes before midnight and Rebecca was due to be released without charge no later than eight o'clock the following morning. So, in real terms, they had less than eight hours left to find McDermott.

So far, all reports had drawn a blank. The porter at the BRI told them that the last he'd seen of McDermott was when he walked down Marlborough Street. After that, he'd simply disappeared. Gone.

"Without McDermott, we haven't got a case," said Karen as she slammed the coffee cup down hard on her desk. "His evidence is pivotal. I even got the bloody CPS to agree to a lighter sentence providing he turned Queen's evidence. Shit! Where the hell is, he?"

Christi's mobile phone rang and on the line was her husband, Mike. "Hi Mike, yes I'm leaving in a bit, just going over a few things with Karen, I won't be long. Give the girls a big kiss for me. Yeah, I love you too, byeee."

Karen, who had only recently gone through a bitter and costly divorce, felt a little envious and secretly wished she had someone calling her. But then someone did, and this someone was calling late at night and on her office line.

"DCI Cook speaking, how can I help you?" she said, hoping they'd found McDermott. Christi sat the other side of her untidy desk going over the CPS report for the fifth time.

A few seconds later, her tired face turned a whiter shade of pale. She held her hand to her mouth, letting out a shriek like a banshee as she held the phone closer to her ear, all the time exclaiming "No! No!"

A few minutes spent nodding her head, she finally said, "Thank you for letting me know Sergeant Steele. Yes, I will, and goodnight." She placed the phone back down on the receiver.

Karen felt as sick as a dog. Christi ran over and put her arm around her shoulder.

"What's happened guv?" she asked. "What was said?" Karen stared back at her for a moment as if in a trance, then tears began to run down her face.

"Close the case Christi. They've just found McDermott's body. Well, they're pretty sure it's him as his head has been hacked off and placed under his arm. His hip flask with the words *Top Bobby* on it has been stuffed in his mouth and his body skinned from the waist down."

Christi was speechless and just held her hands to her mouth imagining the sight of McDermott's stricken body in a pile on the floor. Christi's thoughts went out to McDermott's daughter, Kate, and how someone, even herself, should personally and break the news.

"Have the family been informed?" she asked Karen, close to tears.

Karen looked back at Christi nonsensically, still deep in shock. Then said, "No need Christi, his body was found wrapped in a bin liner outside his ex-wife's house. His daughter apparently found it as she was putting the cat out…

32. Archie.

Leyhill open prison was set in the middle of its own fifteen acres of grounds in idyllic surroundings on the of edge of the village of Cromhall in Gloucestershire. It was rumoured to be a *cosy* and easy place for a convict to serve the final part of his sentence. Some of the more trusted prisoners, the *trustees* as they were known, were allowed home visits once a month. They were even able to grow their own vegetables and sell them for a profit in the prison's well-stocked farm shop. So, life at Leyhill was a long way away from breaking rocks or sewing up mail bags and being banged up twenty-three hours a day.

But Archie Cunningham didn't see it like that. Oh no, because he was an innocent man he refused to conform or become institutionalised. So, from day one, he'd flatly spurned taking part in any of the activities the other prisoners enjoyed. The daily routine of cleaning, followed by a hearty breakfast or attending to a patch of a five by five metre garden the Queen had so generously allotted, simply disgusted him.

Archie would much prefer to just lay on his bed in his twin room he shared with Malcolm, a convicted murderer finishing his life sentence for topping a gay man who'd approached him in a nightclub offering sex at a substantially discounted rate. Malcolm and Archie did not get along. Malcolm only spoke to Archie about one topic – when he asked where he'd hidden the two hundred and fifty grand he'd stolen. Malcolm didn't like ex-coppers and he hated Archie, and Archie in turn hated breathing the same air as Malcolm.

On the odd occasion when he did venture out of his room, he'd spend time wandering the vast grounds, reading his case file out loud to himself, going over and over every detail of how he'd been convicted and then sentenced to six and a half years, despite the money never being recovered.

His brief, the renowned Queen's Council, the Honourable Arthur J Wallis QC, at the time had advised him to plead guilty. But Archie would have never done that. He'd spent the best part of his life savings, a tidy sum of over seventy thousand pounds, defending himself when it would have been so easy to just roll over and take a lighter sentence. But he hadn't. And that was why he'd spent the last six months wandering the grounds, grunting at other inmates instead of conforming, offering a false good morning, or even faking a smile.

As he was making his way back to "B" Block, a terrapin he'd occupied since first arriving at Leyhill, he was stopped in mid-stride by the only man he considered to be a true friend in the entire place, Senior Officer Brian Rigg.

"Archie, there's a visitor here to see you. It's your solicitor, said his name was a Miles... something or other."

"Miles Denton," Archie replied... "Miles Denton, Mr Rigg."

"Well, he's down at the gatehouse waiting to see you. He looks a bit ruffled though, like he's bursting to tell you something. Reckon you ought to get down there straightaway. Hope it's not bad news Archie."

"Me too, thanks Mr Rigg. If I ever get out of here, I'll be sure to repay your kindness somehow."

Riggy or *Big Bri*, as he was affectionately known amongst the other convicts and officers alike, was a good sort, the type of chap who didn't judge a book by its cover and he'd never judged Archie. They'd become firm friends. Many a time Riggy would bring in a homemade fruit cake his wife had made or a few cigarettes so Archie could exchange them for

306

sweets, DVDs or anything that might take his fancy in the prison shop. They'd spend hours together repeatedly going over the case and Riggy would patiently listen as Archie described everything that had happened right down to the finest detail.

Archie quickened his pace as he made his way over to the gatehouse. Upon entering, he was subjected to the customary pat down search and then allowed to enter what the Home Office had so unimaginatively christened the *visitor's suite*.

Miles Denton stood up and scraped the wooden chair back across the tiled floor as he offered his hand across the desk. Then swallowing hard, he began.

"Please take a seat Archie. I'm afraid I have some bad news for you. I also have some very good news, so please just sit and listen for a moment."

Archie pulled out the chair opposite, sat down and nudged himself closer as she started to listen to what Miles Denton had to say.

"Firstly, let's get the bad news out of the way Archie. I'm afraid your last employer, Mrs Enid Williams, was found dead just over a week ago. Apparently, it was natural causes, but no doubt brought on by the theft of her life savings."

Denton paused, looking across the desk at Archie. As a defence lawyer, it didn't bother him who he represented as long as they paid. After all, he could never be quite sure they were innocent. He studied Archie's reaction for a moment and that reaction didn't take long to arrive. His head dropped to his hands and he began to openly sob like a child who'd just lost a parent. And Miles Denton had found his answer.

It took another ten minutes for Archie to console himself, aided by the occasional pat on the shoulder and a few encouraging words by his friend and confidant, Senior Officer Rigg, who had entered the room and was sat beside him.

"I'm really sorry mate," Riggy said, "I know what she meant to you. Let me get you a coffee."

"You also said you had some good news Mr Denton," Archie said, wiping the last tear from his eye. "Let's have it then," he bravely declared, "I could do with some good news after that."

Miles sat forward in his chair, holding both Archie's hands flat on the desk. He looked into his eyes smiling and proudly announced, "You're going to be released Archie! Yes, released! I've managed to arrange bail while I prepare your appeal. The Judge said he believed the grounds for appeal were very strong and your flight risk was minimal. So, you're free to go Archie, a free man and I think…"

Archie was in a dream. He was listening but seemed more interested in gazing out the window at the main gate and the free world only a few yards the other side. He was in shock as Officer Rigg passed him the coffee, his quivering hands spilling some of its contents onto the wooden table. *Enid's dead, I'm free. But where will I go?* he thought.

But deep down Archie already knew where he was going as Senior Officer Rigg congratulated him with a light tap on the shoulder. He got to his feet and asked the desk officer to hand him a set of release papers…

33. Pauly (Moo) Smart

Rebecca sat bolt upright up in her cot. She had been woken by the rattling of keys in her cell door as it swung open and silhouetted in the stark grey doorway was Detective Sergeant Steele.

"Okay Miss Thorneycroft, I have some good news for you. You are going to be released without charge. A Mr Paul Smart is waiting for you in reception."

Rebecca rubbed her grainy eyes wondering if she was dreaming. The WPC on duty had purposely left the fluorescent light on all night and the Sergeant's face was just a blur, a distorted menace made up of yellowing skin and bone. She rubbed her eyes again as she tried to focus and listen as he repeated himself.

"Come on, you heard me!" he said much more sternly this time. He slung her starched white underwear, black skirt and white blouse across the cell. "You're being released, so put your bloody clothes on. I'll be back in a few minutes."

The cell door slammed shut and once more she was alone, sitting on the thin plastic mattress listening as the Sergeant's footfalls dissipated down the corridor.

Five minutes later it was swung open again and the angry Sergeant was standing, gesturing with his hand for her to leave.

"Out! Come on out!" he shouted, pointing his thumb to the corridor behind. "And this is strictly off the record Miss fuckin' Thorneycroft! I don't believe a word you've said! So, you keep looking over that pretty little shoulder of yours because one day I'll be right behind you with an arrest warrant."

But Rebecca was completely unperturbed and lacking fear or submission simply replied, "You can kiss my fuckin' ass Sergeant Steele, and that is also strictly off the record." She confidently strolled away, passed blowing an air kiss as she went.

The livid, seething Sergeant had to refrain himself from lashing out, but he was too late. By then, Rebecca had whisked passed him and was waiting at the door at the end.

As she walked through the door, the tall desk Sergeant who'd originally taken her into custody was standing behind the desk like a puffed-out peacock, with his chest out and his hands on his hips. Sat on a bench opposite was the unmistakeable shape of Pauly Moo grinning like a Cheshire cat and scratching his head like he always did when he felt excited or nervous.

Rebecca immediately ran over to him. Pauly stood up and wrapped his huge bear-like arms around her, lifting her off the ground and swinging her around like a toy. His grip was immense. The bond they shared was pure and unquenchable as tears ran freely down their cheeks.

"Okay! that's enough of that bloody nonsense. This is a police station, not a bloody brothel!" the desk Sergeant broadly announced from the other side of the desk, his thunderous roar causing everyone in the reception to stop what they were doing, including the WPC who'd only just finished typing out Rebecca's release papers at the back of the room.

"Sign here," the Sergeant demanded, sliding a piece of paper across the desk towards Rebecca.

Untangling herself from Pauly's embrace, she walked over slamming her eyes nonchalantly and glaring at the Sergeant before signing the document and rolling the pen back across the desk in one last act of defiance.

"Bye Sergeant," she said, pouting her lips. "I doubt very much we'll ever meet again," She confidently declared as Pauly punched the air and let out a loud "whooping" noise. They both turned and walked through the doors, out into the glorious morning sunshine.

Rebecca had been held in custody for every second of the *ninety-six* hours. In other words, four days and four whole nights. The glare of the sun warmed her face and the electric gates that had so utterly terrified her when she'd entered slid slowly across and finally, she was free.

Pauly had guessed that Rebecca still hadn't passed her driving test, so he'd hired a little Fiat 500C at Bristol airport, his immense frame taking up nearly the whole of the front seats. She loved his slick backed fashionable *skin fade* haircut, with his gleaming white enamel teeth accentuating his natural good looks. But it wasn't just that. No, it was so much more than that. It was his solid good nature and his kindness she adored the most.

"So, Becks, where shall we go, the worlds your oyster?" Pauly cheerfully proclaimed. "Your wish is my command." As he pushed the sliding roof button, the inrush of air almost took their breath away.

"Well, I don't have anywhere to go Pauly. I can't go back to McDermott's, so…."

"Hold on Becks," Pauly said, looking at her confused. "For one, I haven't got a clue who McDermott is! You'll need to tell me the whole story later when we're alone. It can wait, just enjoy the moment. I've booked a room for us for a couple of nights at Jury's hotel in the city centre. So, it's all taken care of. Oh, and after that, you're flying back to Javea with me. I could do with a pretty little manageress like you behind the bar."

Rebecca clapped her hands and, laughing into the wind, shouted, "I love you Pauly! I really do! Tell you what, let's go to the Downs and have a burger shall we?" she asked him. "I'm starving," she said. "Even a McDonalds tastes like shit in prison."

Pauly headed up Park Street and, a quarter of an hour later, they pulled up at a burger bar not far from the old water tower

314

where McDermott had met the infamous Binnie Walters weeks before.

"Come on, the burgers are on me!" Pauly cheerfully announced as he got out of the car, playfully adding, "I bet you're bloody skint as usual."

"Well actually I'm not, so that's where you're wrong for once" was Rebecca's brusque retort as she slammed the passenger door. "Okay, right at this moment I don't have enough money to buy you a burger! she sniggered, "But I do have rather a lot stashed away."

"Ooooh have you now!" Pauly boldly declared, remembering what Symes had told him about helping her out with her *finances,* as he'd termed it.

"Two teas and a couple of hamburgers, one with extra onions please," Pauly ordered as they reached the burger van, smiling as he pointed at Rebecca. "I think I've picked up a damsel in distress."

Rebecca thought his joking repertoire just about summed up her life and laughed. But beneath the false façade, she was deep in thought trying to decide on the best way to explain to him, her best friend, that she was a murderer, a thief, a liar and so much more. Walking towards a bench seat opposite the burger van, Rebecca began her story.

"You see Pauly, I've never lied to you, have I? You're the only one I've never lied to" she said, "And the only person I've ever trusted. I need to tell you a story. It's not a very nice story but I have to tell you, anyway. So, please just try to listen and not say anything until I'm finished. Okay?"

Imitating the character *mini-me*, Pauly put his little finger to his mouth and squeaked through his reply "Okay Becks," he said, as they both laughed remembering how he'd always used do that at Pendleton if she felt down, afraid or alone.

Pauly tore a strip from the top of the paper sleeve and poured the first of two sugars into both teas. Rebecca took a hungry bite of her burger as they both sat on the bench wondering at the beauty of the parkland the Bristol people had christened the *Downs*.

Typically, at the forefront of Rebecca's mind was her favourite subject – money! She began her story, describing how her stepfather, Tom Thorneycroft, poisoned Aunt Mae and how Dominic Symes had forged her will. Then, how she had gone on to steal the gold coins from Wilf and very cleverly dispatched him with a nut curry.

She paused to take another bite of her burger before proceeding to tell him how she'd stolen the best part of a hundred and seventy-five thousand pounds out of Enid's safe. Then, almost as an afterthought, she lied by telling him how she'd planned the whole thing herself and how clever she'd been to make it appear as though Archie had stolen the money. Rebecca laughed as she described every ghastly, lurid detail.

Becoming more serious, Rebecca told him about McDermott, how he'd swindled her out of the real value of the coins and that he was blackmailing her. Finally, she recounted how McDermott had got her in his car one freezing afternoon and savagely raped her. And, although the day was warm and dry and for once and the sun was making an appearance in the sky, Pauly shuddered as he tried to absorb every vicious detail, listening intently as every word tore into his emotions.

He felt split between his loyalty for Rebecca and the disgust at the way she'd so unashamedly described how she had schemed, robbed, even murdered her way to what she so openly termed her ultimate dream – her freedom!

"You see, I'm a free agent now," she announced, as though she'd read his thoughts. "We can go anywhere we want to now. I've hidden the cash and the diamonds in the only place where I knew the police wouldn't look."

"Go on then, where's that then?" Pauly asked, looking into the distance, still clearly shaken by her confession, as he took a last sip of his tea.

"I've hidden it inside the old Betamax machine inside Archie's shed. It was obvious the police would turn the house upside down looking for the money. But somehow, I knew they wouldn't look in there. So, really clever of me don't you think?"

"Yes, Becks, you always were clever. I just didn't realise how clever."

Rebecca wasn't sure if Pauly's reply contained a hint of sarcasm, but decided he was jesting and was proud of her in his own way. She swallowed the last of her burger.

"So, how are *you* going to get in there without being seen to retrieve the money then?" he asked, in an attempt to distance himself by using the singular *you* instead of the plural *we.*

"Well, that's the easy part," Rebecca boastfully replied. "Because Enid's dead, Archie's locked up in prison and I've still got a set of keys to the gates," she said, dangling them in front of his face.

"You see, the cameras outside are really old and they aren't infra-red, so all *we* have to do is nip in at night under the cover of darkness, grab the cash and then we're off to sunny Spain. What do you think?"

Pauly was deep in thought, feeling confused and wondering if, after all she'd been through in her life, she'd gone completely mad. But his sense of loyalty and their bond was just too strong. He looked at her and held out his hand.

"Sounds like *we've* got a deal then," he said, "How much did you say you've got stashed in the tape machine?"

"I didn't, but it's a little over a hundred and forty thousand in cash, and there's still the money I have got in the bank. I have another forty grand left over from Aunt Mae's inheritance, that's after paying off Symes, Tom fuckin' Thorneycroft and that greedy bastard, McDermott. So, I don't want to be a manageress! No, Pauly, I want us to be partners," she boldly and excitedly declared. Pauly didn't react. He just smiled as he wondered what Brett, his husband, might think of that idea.

Finally, after about an hour of listening to more unnerving and disturbing facts, and a detailed description of how Tom Thorneycroft had abused her as a child, Pauly held his head in his hands. His thoughts were elsewhere.

Rebecca found him distant somehow. Gone was the cheerful and playful Pauly. *I've upset him*, she thought as she reached across to touch his hand. He pulled away, lifted his head and stared at her with contempt.

"What's wrong Pauly?" she pleaded. "I'm sorry, I should never have told you, should I?"

He continued to stare at her. His face was lined and taught, and his eyes were glazed. He had a strange distant glare as if he didn't know who she was. He sat looking deeper and deeper at her as though he was exploring her soul.

"Shit! Shit!" she shrieked, causing the burger man to stop what he was doing and look over in alarm. "I think he's having one of his turns!" she shouted, as Pauly shuffled himself closer along the wooden bench.

"It's okay Rebecca. Gilbert loves you, he told me," he whispered as his hands tightened around hers.

Rebecca recoiled, got to her feet and screamed. The concerned burger man shouted across, "Are you all right over there love?" Then, Pauly changed again, disturbed by the burger man shouting. He simply smiled unexpectedly and said, "You'll never change Becks. You always were different. Never mind, let's get a move on we've got a lot of money to collect..."

A shiver ran down Rebecca's spine...

34. Archie

Archie felt for the keys in his jacket pocket, tutting to himself as he looked at Lonsdale and the once immaculate drive now covered in leaves and all manner of detritus and debris. Some idiot had even thrown a Coke bottle over and it was rolling backwards and forwards in the breeze. The great house lay in darkness and the once welcoming façade seemed almost threatening to him as the twin motors on the gates hummed and activated, scraping themselves across the metal guides as he walked though.

It was just after midnight and the great willow trees swayed wistfully in the breeze either side of the long gravel drive as he made his way around the side of the house to the lawn at the rear. His bed for the night was going to be his old armchair, the one Enid had given him twenty years ago, and his pillow was going to be his jacket.

The old timber door to his shed creaked and moaned its way open as he walked through the opening and immediately noticed that the video recorder's red light was still on. *We've got power then, that's something at least*, he thought as he pulled the light switch down and the single bulb dangling above his head immediately coloured the timber slatted walls a deep orangey-red. He blew warm air into his cupped hands, rubbed them together in the cold and wondered to himself if it might be warmer outside than in.

As he sat down and made himself as comfortable as he could in the old armchair, he leant down and plugged the single-bar electric fire into the socket below and the warmth travelled the length of his cold arms.

"How the hell did I end up like this at my age?" he asked himself under his breath, looking around at the bleak surroundings.

"Never mind," he whispered, "You've been in tighter spots than this Archie Cunningham. You'll get through this."

Archie looked down at the old Betamax machine on the desk in front of him, noticing that the LED (on-off) light was flickering. *Must be a loose bulb*, he thought as he checked the tape slot, pushing it open with his index finger and taking a look inside. He could see nothing but a load of old workings and wiring, so he smoothed the top of the old machine like an old friend.

It would have had the answer, but the answer had been removed. Then, as his fingertips crept along the shiny surface, he noticed that two of the tiny black screws were missing. He could feel the indents where they'd been with his thumb. He picked up the heavy machine and shook it. It felt heavier somehow. The red light went out as the mains power cord at the back detached itself as he continued to rock it from side to side. Something was moving around inside. He reached across the desk, opened a drawer and pulled out his screwdriver. The same one he'd used to install the system all those years before.

Gently, one by one, he removed the remaining screws, careful to place them in order on the bench. Finally, he undid the side fixings and placed the screwdriver back in the top drawer.

Using both hands, he struggled with the thin metal top. The front part gave way and, as he was looking closer, he gasped as he realised that someone had stripped out the insides of the machine. That somebody had very cleverly left the mains supply intact so that the tell-tale red light remained on. *So that's why it was flickering*, he thought to himself. As he slid the lid further towards him, he discovered pile after pile of neatly packed money, each one with the give-away *Coutts* bank sleeve still attached.

"If it's the last thing I do, I'll see you swing for this Rebecca bloody Thorneycroft," Archie shouted to himself, thinking he was alone.

"Oh no, you won't Archie" came a reply from behind like something out of a pantomime. A stunned Archie looked around at the orangey silhouette of Rebecca standing by the door and beside her was a huge man he'd never set eyes on before.

"What the hell!" Archie exclaimed, reaching across to open the drawer containing his ball pane hammer. But Rebecca was too fast, too young for him. She dashed across the small room, slamming the drawer shut and catching his fingers in the process. Archie screamed in agony.

"Help! Help!" Archie bellowed as the man moved effortlessly across the room towards him. He stopped midway between Archie and Rebecca staring at Archie's bloodied fingers.

The man's face was ashen, his look ghoulish. He noticed the money and his sunken eyes betrayed a madness that Rebecca had witnessed only a few hours earlier.

"Go on Pauly, hit him," Rebecca shouted in an attempt to slap him out of his trance. "Hit him now then we'll tie him up," she said as he looked in silence, still watching.

Archie had his back to the wall trying to protect himself with his hands and, despite his age and weakness of limb, he made a quick dash and tried to push past the man's huge frame. But it wasn't possible, Pauly was too big, too strong. He threw Archie backwards like a mannequin against the bench, smashing his head into the shed's strong timber support. Calmly, without reflection or utterance, he grabbed hold of Archie's lapels and slammed his head downwards onto the wooden bench below.

Rebecca screamed as thick red blood pumped from Archie's ears, nose and mouth as he lay quite listless and still like a rag doll. He was quite dead.

There was silence. Pauly stood with his back to Rebecca. All she could see or hear was his laboured breaths and the huge muscles on his shoulders moving in and out as he looked down at Archie's limp body. Rebecca froze. *It wasn't meant to happen this way,* she thought. *All he had to do was knock him out, tie him up and they'd be off, free.*

Pauly looked around and then directly at her. She realised it wasn't Pauly standing in front of her. It was the man she'd sat beside on the Downs earlier that day. Someone called Gilbert!

"Are you frightened Rebecca? I'm not. Not anymore, I'm not," Gilbert said, shooting her an alarming stare. "This money belongs to me Rebecca! And, if you knew me you would know I do not like to share. They used to beat me in Pendleton, you know. In the sin bin."

Rebecca took two steps back reaching the door, but she was too late to reach the handle. Gilbert surged across the room faster than a praying mantis and smashed her to the floor with a back hand, followed by an uppercut that cracked her jaw like a wrecking ball. As she fell to the floor, her last conscious memory was Gilbert yanking on one of her stiletto heels. The mortal world dissolved around her.

And Gilbert stood over her…

35. Christi

The oxygen mask around her injured face felt tight, her jaw was smashed, her left eye was hanging by a thread and resting on her cheek. The ambulance wailed its alarm as it travelled at speeds of over seventy miles an hour en route to the BRI hospital in Bristol.

DI Christi Blake was on the green bench opposite looking across at Rebecca and watching her drift from this world to the other. Two paramedics were working tirelessly, one at each end of her body, taking turns in swapping IVs and applying pressure to the numerous tears and cuts adorning her once beautiful face, arms and upper body.

Although Christi had followed this woman tirelessly for the past six months, her thoughts were conflicted and alternated between a natural desire to help the casualty and those of wishing that this particular victim would die a thousand deaths right in front of her. Rebecca slipped in and out of consciousness.

If it hadn't been for the anonymous phone call from a passer-by, Christi was aware that she'd still be studying Rebecca's file, still be looking for that small and as yet unseen clue that might lead to her conviction. But that was all in the past thanks to that telephone call. She'd caught her red-handed.

It was appalling that it took the life of an innocent ex-copper to finally collar her, but Rebecca's presence at the murder scene was all the evidence she needed.

So, you just live Rebecca… Just live, she thought as the ambulance screeched to a halt outside of the BRI's busy A&E department.

Rebecca spent five night in and out of consciousness, fighting for her life, in intensive care. A uniformed police officer was placed outside her room at all times, not that she would be able to abscond. Since being x-rayed, the doctors had discovered she'd also sustained a broken ankle, a detached retina and a fractured collar bone.

In short, Rebecca was lucky to be alive.

Two weeks later, she was transferred to her own private room, a secure room without a window. Not because she held any notoriety or deserved special treatment but because, despite her appalling injuries, the risk of her escaping was still extremely high.

A few days after her transfer, DCI Karen Cook and DI Christi Blake, carrying a small tape recorder and the all-important file, arrived at the foot of her bed. Rebecca was awake, spoon-feeding herself a bowl of Sugar Puffs bathed in cold milk. Her face was covered in bandages and bruises extending from her once small petite nose to the top of her blue hospital blouse. She looked like she'd aged ten years as her blue and red bruise-covered arm placed the empty dish down on the bedside cabinet.

"So, here we are again then Rebecca," said Karen. "A bit touch and go for a while I must say. You're a tough bird all right. Shame about that pretty little face of yours, don't you think Christi?" Karen remarked as Rebecca pulled herself upright in the bed.

Christi didn't react to her guvnor's bitchy comment. She was simply overwhelmed at the appearance of this once beautiful face now so cruelly defiled and permanently disfigured by what she could only assume was Archie's frenzied defence.

"So, what happens to me now then?" Rebecca asked, attempting to mask an obvious fear in her tone.

Christi and Karen were now sitting either side of the bed and within touching distance of her. The atmosphere in the small room was electric. Rebecca was perspiring, a strong smell of iodine emanating from her pores, as she waited for a response. She asked again, "What happens now?"

In one of her well-rehearsed statements she and Christi had rehearsed earlier, Karen said, "Well Rebecca, you are going to be escorted to a holding facility called Pucklechurch Remand Centre. Once there, you will be charged with the murder of Archibald Reginald Cunningham and you will also be arrested for the theft of over two hundred and fifty thousand pounds in cash from the home of Enid Williams on or before the dates of..."

Rebecca cut in, screaming, "I didn't murder Archie! It was Pauly Moo! He did it, he smashed Archie's head into the bench. I saw it! I'll admit to the money, but I swear I didn't kill him."

Rebecca was close to breaking point. Karen and Christi were aware and just looked at her as if she'd gone completely mad.

"I demand to see a solicitor!" Rebecca spouted, folding her arms in an attempt to regain some composure.

For all the hard work she'd put in, Karen had agreed that Christi should be the one to deliver the punch line. Rebecca's *fait acomplis,* so to speak.

"Well Rebecca, you see, it's not going to be that easy to wriggle out of it this time. You've probably heard about the murder of Detective Sergeant McDermott's by now?"

Gut reaction made Rebecca sit bolt upright in bed, she grimaced from the searing pain from her broken collar bone as it travelled through her body. "Murdered? What do you mean he's been murdered? When? How…?"

"That's none of your concern Rebecca," said Christi cutting in. "Needless to say, he won't be appearing in court as a prosecution witness. So, that should cheer you up, not that we need him now anyway."

Rebecca, although clearly in shock, still had all her wits about her. "That has nothing to do with me. You can't pin that one on me, no more than you can Archie's murder. So, once more, I demand to see a solicitor."

Rebecca folded her arms defiantly and smiled at Christi as she confidently awaited her reply.

"Well, as far as a solicitor is concerned, I suggest you look elsewhere" said Christi leaning towards her. "You see Mr Symes' offices were raided this morning after a tip off from another anonymous source. When his safe was opened, twenty-five thousand pounds in cash wrapped up in an envelope was found. Would you like to guess who's prints were all over that envelope? Go on, Rebecca, take a wild guess."

Rebecca didn't respond straightaway as she needed a moment to think.

"So, what! I've already admitted to nicking the money. What does that prove. Go on arrest me then. I'm guilty," she said symbolically holding out her hands.

But Christi had saved the best for last.

"In time Rebecca, in time," Christi confidently replied. But I think it's time we furnished you with some other facts regarding the murder. So, for the sake of legal compliance and so that you are fully aware of the damning evidence we hold against you. Your stiletto heel, the one missing from your clothing bag, is being subjected to the most detailed forensic tests available after it was found embedded in the eye socket of Mr Archibald Reginald Cunningham. I might add it is covered in your fingerprints and DNA. So, dear, Mr Symes won't be here to help you this time. To coin a phrase Rebecca, get the fuck out of that one!"

Christi inhaled deeply as Karen laughed. Rebecca flung herself back on her pillow screaming at the top of her voice, "it was Pauly Moo." An unperturbed Christi continued, "Oh, and Rebecca, before we leave and the officers escort you to Pucklechurch there's one other thing you need to know.

Christi pulled out her pad and read from it.

"A Mr Latham of Latham Jones and Stringer called the station this morning enquiring as to your whereabouts. He said he had some good news for you. I asked what it was and at first, he was reluctant to spill the beans. When I informed him that you are a prime suspect in a prominent murder investigation, he opened up. Do you know what he said Rebecca? Well, I'll tell you, shall I? Mr Latham said you'd come into some money. He said that an ex-employer of yours, a Mrs Enid Williams, had left you a fifty per-cent share in a house, including its contents, called Lonsdale in Clifton

Heights. The other half was left to Archie Cunningham, the man you murdered. Apparently, according to Mr Latham, the house is worth well in excess of eight million pounds. Such a shame you won't be around to enjoy your new-found wealth Rebecca now the will has been revoked…

The End

For a look at my other books "Salt's War" and "Blood and Country" (Volume 2), please visit amazon.co.uk.

I do hope you enjoyed reading "The Carer" as much as I enjoyed writing it. If this is the case, please be kind enough to leave me a review, or contact me at saltswar@yahoo.com

Printed in Great Britain
by Amazon

81365857R00192